COLLECTION OF AUGURIES

Stories

ANNIE Q. SYED

Printed in the United States of America at McNally Jackson Books, 52 Prince Street, New York, NY 10012.

First Edition

ISBN 978-1-938022-45-6

For my mother and father, my favorite storytellers,
who encouraged my stories.

Acknowledgments

I AM GRATEFUL TO MY FAMILY FOR THEIR LOVE AND support that made this collection possible.

When I began writing these stories in 2010 I didn't have any particular audience in mind. However, I knew with more certainty than I had yet to know anything else that I had to place these stories in a tangible medium instead of thought provoking conversations that dissipate all too quickly. I am grateful that I could create such a digital shelf in the form of my website, and that would not have been possible without the patient, daring, diligent Vusi Sindane, director of www.donebyexperts.com.

I continued to use my website as a writing portfolio and I am very grateful to all the readers of my "blog" who have sincerely supported my writings from the very beginning. It is because of these readers I continued to write beyond the noise of agents, publishers, self-publishing, digital publishing etc. It is through their support that I continued to recall there existed a realm where stories were told when your grandmother was rubbing oil in your hair...where stories were shared under big jacaranda trees in South Africa about the color purple and dreams inside bones...stories under the vast Arabian sky, where a father took the time to point at stars…it is through them that I held steadfast to the belief that once upon a time people really cared to hear a good story.

We constantly watch stories being churned in our thoughts, a big, wild mixer of memories, dreams, imagination, not to mention the constant to and fro of past and future of which most of us are not even aware lest we stop to pay attention to our breath where it all dissolves into the fraction of now. And to breathe like that requires a dedicated practice, not just a carved out time for meditation or yoga, although a consistent practice of such dedication eventually seeps into those moments when we are not practicing yoga or meditating, so it becomes very much like breathing indeed, you are doing it without thinking! To this end, I am grateful for my yoga practice with my instructor Marco Rojas in New York City, which helped me to use my imagination beyond my thoughts.

This collection literally would not have been possible without the support of Jamie Berry (www.jamieberry.com); feedback and literary friendship of Lucy Pollard-Gott (http://fictional100.wordpress.com/); and the hardworking and patient Beth at McNally Jackson Books in SoHo, New York City.

I am grateful for my closest friends who have unconditionally supported my writing efforts long before my website was created. I am truly blessed to have had so many people, some strangers and others who have known me for more than two decades, who encouraged---and believed in---these stories before I did.

Last but not least, I must mention Jimmy Wales, founder of Wikipedia, the largest reference website, which supplemented research for these stories. I am grateful to all the contributors who relentlessly edit and update the information for accuracy.

Contents

DaVinci Dreams

Thais Stories

Foreword

THESE LUMINOUS, PRISMATIC TALES BY ANNIE Q. SYED evoke the chain of stories hidden in the present moment. With their immediacy of dialogue, sure anchoring in place, and gift for original metaphor, they show how dreams and everyday portents--Auguries--beg to be understood and transform the dreamer.

Some stories are short, energetic frissons to shake the mind, emotions, and senses out of their usual ruts; they prove both disquieting and thrilling. Others are longer explorations of territory ranging from modern neuropsychology to Egyptian mythology, beautifully interconnected by themes of memory, identity, and the phantom bits of consciousness that reappear in our dreams. Some characters face traumas that seem to sever parts of self or soul, but they also encounter mystery, the unexpected intrusions of love and wisdom that may knit their personal histories back together. This collection is an exciting debut from a powerful narrative voice, mythic in resonance, yet thoroughly modern.

—Lucy Pollard-Gott, author of *The Fictional 100*

Note to the Reader

WE ARE ALL STORYTELLERS. We live our lives in and through stories as though this imaginary axis on which our planet rotates is made up of stories.

Storytelling is an old oral tradition passed down from generation to generation, from Irish folklore to Arabian nights to African healing to Native American songs and so on. Now we have formulas for storytelling, which would be fine if one took on the responsibilities that used to come with that tradition.

A storyteller leaves permanent imprints that are only replaced by new imprints. When speaking, one keeps on adding layers of facts as they are 'delivered' where as, when writing, the writer sculpts words that have no meaning until you place them in a context that satisfies the writer's imagination as much as possible to reach some intended reader. Often a writer even makes up stories where to a storyteller, dear reader, stories just "come." They can come in the form of others divulging more than is necessary out of whatever compulsion; they can come in the form of dreams; they can be passed down fragments overheard from one's ancestors. A storyteller remains cognizant that he or she is just a conduit.

According to my current understanding of a storyteller (coming from a culture of such traditions), I must admit that both the storyteller and the writer carry wounds, some personal, some—often—others'. They are soldiers in a perpetual war for understanding. The wound deserves the writer's attention too, for the storyteller is the surgeon but the writer must put the cast on the permanent fractures. The storyteller is not concerned with politic. The writer, the writer as an artist, must be; for even love is a political act, because even love can stir a cultural revolution!

Stories are threads that weave us to one another. We suffer now as never before because we as a people everywhere have stopped sharing stories or have safely boxed and labeled our stories for the relating of particular ethnicities, cultures, religions, regions etc. The pop culture of "Reality Television" and "social media" attempted to create a generic medium of world wide connecting, unsuccessfully. It certainly feels revelatory of another's most personal life but we view these stories as spectators in the shallow end without knowing where the deep end begins, often those who are emotional exhibitionists flaunting their melodrama rarely know the deep end themselves, looping the circumference of the inferno that burns within. Showing is not sharing. A *telling* that stirs something within yourself and another is sharing. Just like slicing a thin layer of the cornea cannot be done without a slight flinching for the onlooker and the one on whom the eye surgery is performed, so is the case with truly sharing—both feel the pinch of a truth no matter how far removed. We have convinced ourselves that what is offered through pop culture and instant "social networking" provides a sufficient view into the colorful tapestry that is our being. Although this cursory sharing does create a dull reverberation within, in actuality, it merely tugs a stray piece of the thread, whereupon there are many other vital strands creating the fabric of our cosmos. Our collective humanity trembles; the grand picture remains blurry as we continue our search, not realizing that the more authentically and widely we share our stories, the tighter the tug that creates cross-stitches that eventually reveal the picture we seek.

The most enduring hindrance for any writer is that it's all been written before. Anyone who feels compelled must write because people forget! Every story that has ever been written carries with it the messages we are all looking for since the beginning of time, every author carries the same light (and burden) to share what some have forgotten or what some still do not quite understand. The reason those who choose to write, even when they write the same stories that have been told before, is because ultimately the writer hopes, that maybe, just maybe, this time around this writer's words will reach where all else failed before.

I write with the liberty that I do because over time these stories have become mine. My hope is they will become yours too. No story, like no individual, stands alone in this world. A dim flicker shines through the fractured spaces in these living apparitions' tales, serving as a guide for treading upon expansive realms deep within ourselves where we are afraid to venture alone.

Auguries
plural of au·gu·ry (Noun)

1. A sign of what will happen in the future; an omen

2. The work of an augur; the interpretation of omens

Stories

"Life is a festival, for all who know about it"
—Ethan Holub

"Why do you call him XYZ?"

"His initials."

She anticipated Franz to continue.

"Xavier Zurbruck."

"What does the Y stand for?"

"I dun-no. I just added that. Made sense. To apply the finishing touches to the X. Z. initials."

"Really?"

Actually, I am not sure if any part of his name is Xavier or Zurbruck.

"I like Mr. X. Y. Z. It makes for a good story. And unique initials."

Yes, we like stories.

"You think he is crazy? He just stands there. *Every single day.* In his bright white outfit with white paint on his face," said Tariro, staring at the still poised man, planted in the middle of the market square, dressed in bleached white, as if furnishing a silent benediction for bystanders.

Franz didn't answer.

A woman, a blur of a bright yellow suit rushed past them, shrieking broken German to whoever was on the other end of her mobile phone, without even noticing X.Y.Z.

"He is not crazy. I spoke to him once. He does this to soak up people's stories," Franz said finally.

"What do you mean soak up? He *talks* to people? *They* talk to him?" asked Tariro. "I thought he just stood there silently. Every time we have seen him that's what it seems like, no? With a weird gesture that changes randomly. One hand up, the other on his stomach. Or remember last week—one hand up, index finger on his lips, and the other hand on his hips?" Tariro continued with an amused interest.

Franz began, "Well, he didn't speak to me while he is doing his *thing*. Just ran into him near the post office once, some months ago. Didn't really recognize him without the paint on his face, but somehow I knew it was him."

"How?"

"I just did," Franz replied and shrugged, "Besides, it doesn't matter how, because he quickly confirmed that yes, he is the guy in white from the market place."

Tariro enjoyed her time with Franz. He was a fifty-five year old tailor, owner of the shop "Stitch in Time" that employed three seamstresses, one from India and the other two from Pakistan, part of Germany's emigrant citizenry. Yet Franz introduced himself as a writer the first time they met six months ago. Tariro, only a visitor, when not working on her dissertation research, would stop by "Stitch in Time" and they would walk over to the market place and sit on a bench.

The first time Franz told her a story it was about Kristiane Sarah. Kristiane's husband left her for another woman who made better German Potato Casserole. Upon hearing this, Tariro cried. Franz tried to comfort her by stating, "It's *all* about the *proportion* of the Worcestershire sauce *to* the tablespoons of cider vinegar." Tariro smiled—she just missed home.

Franz shared with her that he was a widow without any children and simply knew a lot of people and their stories. Tariro, too shy to speak to strangers or befriend others in her seminars, considered these stories background information for when she would finally gather the courage and time to meet the people who owned the anecdotes. She disregarded that knowing how she was, such a time wouldn't come.

"So tell me—what is X.Y.Z.'s story then?"

"It's a short one. He is not a man of many words. He was coming out of the post office and just abruptly began talking to me."

"Wait—you said *you* spoke to him?"

"Oh Tari-ro. Does it matter?" It was at this moment that Franz reminded Tariro of her uncle back home, even though neither her uncle nor she belonged in the same pigment spectrum as Franz.

"No. I suppose not," Tariro said. "Please, continue," she said extra politely.

"Well—he said that he stands there every week-day to snort in people's stories. That people think he is not listening but he listens to everyone. And they don't realize this is why they feel better when they walk past him. Their amusement is actually a relief—they have unloaded a story unto him."

Tariro stared at Franz. She didn't know how to tell Franz this didn't make sense to her, that this meant X.Y.Z. was crazy.

"But Franz," Tariro spoke quietly, for the first time considering X.Y.Z. as a man who could possibly hear them and not just a breathing statue for staring at, "People don't really talk to him—they talk to each other while near him."

"So?!" Franz exclaimed.

"Well, so…"

"You know people don't really listen to one an-other. They only hear half. Half what they want and half what is being said," said Franz matter-of-factly. Then continued, "So X.Y.Z. absorbs in the half that is not heard but needs to be."

Tariro was quiet. She looked at the old man stand-ing still in the middle of the market square, as if rooted into the ground, whitewashed—white hair, white gar-ments, white gloves, white shoes.

Tariro and Franz walked away from the market square quietly. She gave him a hug before they parted for opposite routes.

While walking back to her flat, processing memories intertwined with distorted imagination, she thought of calling her husband the next day, standing within earshot of X.Y.Z. She wanted someone to hear the other story of why she needed to get away.

Franz returned to an empty home, regretting like he did every night, that he should have never divorced his wife for some woman that didn't even like *this* Germany. He opened his notebook and jotted the letters *x, y,* and *z* followed by a question mark. Tomorrow he would go to the post office to see if maybe there was something from his sons in the mail. He got ready for bed as he thought about his wife's German Potato Casserole.

There are stories that make us and then there are stories we make up.

Every weekday morning, exactly at 6:00 a.m., Mr. Erim gets up to a barely audible alarm that comes from a clock purchased in Verona, Italy in 1983 by his wife. He slowly sits up and stares at the tile floor, reaching his feet for the plastic slippers he picked at a donation center not far from the local post office. Every weekday morning, he reminds himself, aloud, "Must stop by the post." Thereafter, he walks, dragging the tightness in his joints, to the bathroom which smells of rotten cranberries and mold, even though there is no mold. Mr. Erim watches the tap water run and collect just the right amount of hotwarm in the sink while he prepares to shave.

Mr. Erim wishes there was a window in the bath-

room, even though it would still not provide access to natural light. "Man needs to know there is air out there," he would tell Clarise, his ex-wife who left him when all his companies collapsed along with his lucid interpretations of reality, fifteen years ago.

After shaving, he combs what little is left of his white hair. Then he gently places white paint on his face, like aftershave, to blend his face with the rest of his white outfit. While the white paint dries he looks for his white gloves. Fifteen years ago, he had a melt down and got on his knees to pray only to realize praying was not enough. Ever since then he has gone to market squares in different cities to sublease his mind so his body can rest.

Pleasure Zone

"WHAT DOES MORAL MEAN?" ZOLAR ASKED ENTHU-SIASTICALLY.

"Your father is not doing *moral* things. Does that give you an idea?" Shaarleen huffed at her eleven-year-old son.

"So not having a steady girlfriend is *not* moral?"

"Don't get smart with me, Zolar." Shaarleen replied quickly.

"I wasn't being smart, Mom. I don't know what it means." And he didn't.

Zolar turned his head to look outside the passenger side window.

After a few minutes had passed, he asserted, "I can see why they call this the land of awes." His eyes continued to follow the specs of greenness between the dry flaxen stretches of prairie fields spilling far into the horizon, opening the sky's mouth even wider. His mother didn't understand the pun because she wasn't listening.

"A girl in my class—she is new, from Trinidad, but Dad's not from Trinidad yet her skin sort of looks like his, but only sort of, like when he has been in the sun—thought it was 'Wizard of o. z.' not 'Wizard of *Oz*.'"

"That's nice."

"There is nothing *nice* about that Mom," Zolar snapped, "Kids made *fun* of her all day cuz she had never heard of Wizard of Oz and said 'o' 'z' instead."

"Well, that's not so nice," Shaarleen replied. Then added, "Shouldn't pay attention to people's skin color."

"Where is Trinidad? Is it named after someone's dad?"

"I don't know Zolar. Somewhere south."

"Well Dad's not from there."

"No he is not. He is from Missouri. *Misery*."

"You are not as funny as dad. Everyone has heard of it being called *Misery*."

Well, funny is all your dad was, laughing his way right out of reality.

Shaarleen turned up the volume on the radio only to hear an advertisement about a furniture sale for the upcoming weekend at a mall in the town she was driving through. It was a town so small she would neither remember having driven past it nor register that even miniature cities were host to malls.

She appreciated how her thoughts slowed down while driving on the interstate. Or perhaps there were so many impenetrable thoughts, all unable to keep pace with the speed limit on the highway, that they began unraveling as just one or two sound bites that repeated intelligibly.

She had tried her best, both in her own and her therapist's perspective, including the long eight-hour drives every other weekend so Zolar could spend time with his father while she stayed with Barb and Will. Shaarleen never knew how uncomfortable it made Zolar's father when she stayed with her friend—*their* old friends.

But now it was different. She now had someone and although she openly declared no one could officially ever take upon the "father" role for Zolar, she had decided she deserved a companion—in and out of bed.

Shaarleen was finally confident that she had made the right decision after the court hearing provided a custody judgment. *A young boy had no business growing up with a father who could never serve as a good role model—not just because he was a drunk—not just because he cheated on me, yes, it counts even if we were separated: I still took on two jobs to support us, how separated is that–*

"Whoa!" Zolar exclaimed. Hijacking her out of her analysis. "What's that place we just passed?"

"What place?" She looked outside.

"*That* place!"

"What place?"

She ignored Zolar's question after having assessed the image in the rearview mirror.

"Didn't you see it? It looked magical with all sorts of lights. Didn't look like a hotel to me. Was it a motel mom? What's the difference between a hotel and a motel, mom?"

Zolar juggled his thoughts with his questions. According to him the hotel was named "Pleasure Zone" because that was what was written on the outside.

"Probably just a run down shack. Don't worry about it," Shaarleen explained, attempting to shift the boy's curiosity away from the bordello exposure. She decided she was never going to take this new route again.

"What's a pleasure zone mom?"

"Zolar! Stop! Just stop! Your father has ruined you! Do you understand?" she screamed. "He has ruined you! Bringing home different women has messed you up! You hear me?!" she continued underneath unexpected sobs, "Do you hear me…"

"I am sorry, Mom. Dad's girlfriends never say anything about a pleasure zone. I didn't know what it was," Zolar said. And he didn't.

"Your dad is self-absorbed. Sick in the head. You understand?! I need you to forget whatever you have seen him do or say! I promise you will be fine once you move in with me for good. He is careless."

"Mom. I have never seen him do anything unmoral but drink beer while he watches T.V. after work. Did I use the word *moral* right, Mom?" Zolar asked. He tried to change the subject, feeling guilty for having upset his mother who was to remain this way for the rest of the ride and until he was well into his thirties.

*

He didn't know, and neither did she, that it had nothing to do with him or even the father but more to do with the uncertainty a single mother accepted in a new relationship. Zolar thought of telling his mother that his father had never brought home any of "the girlfriends" but decided against it for the fear of seeing his mother cry or hearing her scream, or worse, both.

Three weeks later, while watching the sunset through the window behind the television set, Zolar would hear the hushed sounds of a pleasure carved for a man and a woman. Shaarleen and her "new friend," upstairs in her bedroom, explored the inevitable attraction borne between two competing needs and wants.

Zolar stepped outside onto the porch. The sky resembled the day they had taken a new route between two states.

There are places that stay with us long after we have driven past them not because they are prepossessing but because they are reprehensible, but that's not even why, their existence remains incomprehensible.

The phantasmagorical shades of twilight in the sky created while the sun kissed the earth goodbye palliate man made deformities. Zolar decided he was forever going to enjoy sunsets.

Love: Making Music

"WHY DO I HAVE TO KNOW ABOUT BABA IN ORDER TO *UNDERSTAND* YOUR MUSIC?"

"You don't have to *understand* it. And it's not–*my* music. It's music. You don't own music," he replied.

He scanned Odia's long unshaven legs, host to a suntan which highlighted her two bright Kokopelli tattoos, one on each ankle. He wanted to let her go, recycle her back to the Universe, out of his life. Yet she was balm for his reactions to the world, relief for windburned astringent feelings.

"Don't look at my legs," she said childishly, "I need to shave." She grabbed the tattered white blanket over her legs and propped herself against the headboard of his bed.

"Babatunde Olatunji–Baba–was a virtuoso of West African percussion. His 1959 album 'Drums of Passion' was a worldwide sensation, a global hit. He received a Grammy Award in 1991 for his collaboration with Grateful Dead drummer Mickey Hart on their Planet Drum album. He *is* percussion."

"Can you toss over *that* pillow instead?" she asked.

Six months with her and he was already reminiscing about their beginning; he wasn't aware though that this always marked the onset of the end of his relationships.

There is a drum circle on Sundays at Venice Beach in Los Angeles. The orchestration is self-arising. This time it began with one guy and his Tibetan bells and then within minutes the other drummers formed a circle. The percussion sounds challenge the ocean waves in the background for a rhythm. People come and watch and then pass on by. Some Sundays the crowd is intense but small. Other Sundays, despite the overcast sky, the pulsating vibrations are airborne above the boardwalk in a tempo which attracts a congregation.

No one can resist drums.

He recalled Odia staring at him on that particular Sunday when they first met. As a performer he was used to entranced looks. He mistook Odia's interest in him for interest in the music he created. He was certain she could feel the music beyond the swayskip-bouncehop-tripbop in the hips which the magnetic beats compelled.

He told her that very night he met her that he was in love with her. She was genuinely impressed that he knew so much about music, especially drums. She was a regular at all the local spots where small overcrowded spaces boomed eclectic global sounds.

"Okay fine, Babatunde is AWESOME. But I still want you more. So come back here. I get scared that you are going to leave me when you get 'discovered' when you start talking about music like that."

"I fell in love with you because I thought you felt music like I do," he said calmly. He hesitated to get off the couch. From where he was seated he could just examine her as if she was a painting hanging on someone's wall in a corridor. "I read an article once which said that if you say 'I love *because*' it is not really love. That love just is," he continued cautiously.

"What are you saying?' she asked quickly as she sat up, alert, away from the headboard. "You don't love me because you think I don't understand your music?"

"It's not *my* music," he repeated. "I am not going to get 'discovered' like you think I should because I am good or maybe you think that's what I want. Because I don't. I don't want that. I just play to understand energy. Energy of everything around, you know," he continued.

"This understanding of 'not-my-music' is not going to pay bills or advance your career," Odia pointed out without intending to hurt him.

"There is no career, Odia. I just create music," he said, withholding the lurking thought: *didn't have to worry about money before budgeting your nightlife.*

"Talk about this after we go out tonight to that show at Zanzibar?" She stated rather than asked, since she was already on her way to his turquoise tiled bathroom. "Besides, you can still create music, just not on the streets, you know?"

Odia twirled with a head full of thoughts in the shower: how they would return after the night out to make love like many nights before, while listening to some soft drums from Mali or Benin in the background, and he would say what he always said before falling asleep, *love is like making music*, and then fall asleep wrapped around her. They would be fine, she decided.

She didn't know then that she loved how *he* loved music more than she loved him.

"It's not the streets," he said to no one.

Things Left Unsaid

WHAT DO I TELL MY FORTY-TWO YEAR OLD SON ON
THE DISSOLUTION OF HIS MARRIAGE OF SEVEN YEARS?

I have always been a father of a few words: *steady on that bike; careful with the car; don't be at the wrong place at the wrong time; you smoke-since when?; girls are like that; St. Mark's was the best pizza joint then and now; your mother couldn't get it; not sure if that major will get you a real job; you can leave Philly but you will come back...*
Maybe I should have said more.

The living room doesn't seem so large with him asleep on the couch. The black shelves are filled with dvds, videotapes, and CDs. The maroon blankets hang loosely on the shoulders of the suede green couch set which frames the extra large mahogany coffee table. I look at him asleep on the couch. I look outside my high rise condominium building to the tiny cars beneath that move too fast for me to distinguish their makes.

When he was thirteen he divulged his fascination with cities which consisted of two words: *Council Bluffs, Burr Oaks, Three Forks, Los Osos* and others I can't think of the top of my head. He got upset with me when I told him *Truth or Consequences* in New Mexico had three words and not two.

He had a favorite light blue cotton t-shirt, the back of which read "Free Quebec." I recall his sister asking where he got it.

"A friend."

"Can I have it?"

"No."

"Your friend Canadian?"

"No."

I look around the dulled walls which accommodate framed pictures of him and Marlayna growing up, alongside the art collection, some of it my own work, which doesn't quite stir much other than rushed memories of wine in galleries.

"What time is it?" he asks.

"Almost eight."

He turns over onto his side.

"What you thinkin'?"

I remain by the window sill, looking down at children who zig-zag their way between the paths we carve for them.

"About that raggedy blue shirt of yours. You know the one Marlayna took without asking you and then gave it to her then-boyfriend and the fight that followed?" I answer.

"Ha."

I walk over to him.

"Don't worry," he says to me.

"Shouldn't I be the one telling you that?"

"The truth is we should have both worried more."

"About?" I ask him.

"Everything," he says. He gets up to look for his cigarettes.

"I love this house."

"It's an apartment," I remind him, "A house has a backyard."

Neither can make it a home, I think.

"Whatever happened between you and Ma?"

I don't want to be surprised he still asks this.

Relationships are inherently complex, I want to tell him. We try to understand them so as to realize this, not necessarily to make them uncomplicated.

"She couldn't get it," I offer.

Illumination

ARPAD WAS NEITHER A DEVOUT CHURCHGOER NOR A COMMITTED ATHEIST. He devoted his Sunday mornings to a shot of espresso, one cigarette, then another shot of espresso, and then another cigarette. After the second round Arpad would take a short break and look out the smudgy cafe windows until the waitress—Kaitlin, the only one of the three who worked at Cafe V willing to serve him, given he would never as much as say "hello" or "thank you"—would bring him the morning newspaper and scissors.

"The ones my wife owns at home are much better than these shoddy worthless ones," Arpad would say at this point.

Kaitlin had learned two years ago—Arpad had been coming here every Sunday morning as far as she could remember working at Cafe V—to not reply. Two years ago when she had retorted something clever he called her a "gnome who needs a haircut" and had added, "even my wife's scissors could never fix your hair so that anyone would notice you." Although Kaitlin had then told the manager who only showed his face at Cafe V once a month that she was quitting, in fact she never left.

Arpad would then proceed to read the head-lines—only the headlines—from the Sunday paper and then cut out the boxed sections containing comic strips, which he didn't read. Arpad enjoyed carefully cutting along the lines of the comic strip boxes. The concentration required for the precision to move the scissors from one end of the edge to the other eased his anxieties momentarily.

What Arpad did during the rest of the week was without incident: he worked as a part-time car me-chanic in Pest, which is to say he was willing to of-fer a helping hand when someone's car broke down or needed to be jump-started. Others only reached out to him when all other options had been exhausted be-cause no one really knew what he would say when he was thanked.

One time he told a husband and wife visiting Bu-dapest from Germany, "You should have rented bikes. You can't jump-start love."

The German couple recounted this incident with Arpad to their hotel manager after he had politely in-quired why the wife was crying when they had returned to the hotel earlier. The hotel manager was not quite interested in the story about Arpad—whom the locals knew and ignored—but more concerned with the qual-ity of their stay. The German couple was not interested in sharing what Arpad had really said, so the husband replied, "Oh—my wife is just really upset that I rented a cheap car that broke down and then we ran into the rudest man ever that someone had recommended."

Both men nodded and went about their business:

the husband to a wife who wanted to listen to Arpad and the manager who ignored the likes of Arpad in his country.

Of all the days in the year Világítás was the only day Arpad was remotely personable. Világítás, the Day of the Dead, a Day of Remembrance, was his favorite day. Once a year in November he would begin the day—a national holiday—by stopping by the cafe he had been going to and give flowers to the waitress who attended him. If it was a male waiter, he offered flowers for the wife, sister, mother, or grandmother. Prior to knowing Kaitlin, he gave flowers to the woman who worked at Cafe Kossuth Lu, where he used to go on Sundays.

One November he gave flowers to Kaitlin. Kaitlin cried at the gesture and he wanted to tell her she should no longer work at Cafe V. But instead he murmured that he was headed to the small, nameless graveyard in Visegrad, a small village town outside of Budapest, where his wife was buried. Kaitlin couldn't help wishing that every day was Day of the Dead and felt morbid for thinking that.

Kaitlin had replied, "You are a nice man."

Arpad wanted to tell her that she was beautiful and he loved her curly hair that couldn't be contained under a hat, with a rubber band, or any beauty product, but instead he just walked away.

Other than this communication, no other took place between the two of them. That is until the following year in November, also Világítás, when Kaitlin saw him in Kerepesi Temeto—one of the biggest graveyards in Budapest—cleaning out weeds, washing tombstones, and sweeping leaves around the graves, a typical preparation for lighting candles around the cemetery.

Kaitlin walked up to him and said hello. He didn't reply. Kaitlin felt as if he didn't recognize her. She tried speaking to him again and when he didn't reply again she finally said, "I thought your wife was buried in Visegrad. Why are you here?"

"My wife had hair like yours. Lots of big everywhere," Arpad replied.

Kaitlin stared at him, all of a sudden more conscious about her hair than the first time he had called her a gnome.

"I like remembering her here instead of back home," Arpad said.

Kaitlin noticed his dirty hands that had been picking weeds around graves all day.

"My grandparents are buried here," Kaitlin replied, pointing to a corner of the vast cemetery. She continued, "My family should be joining me at night to light candles. I just came a little earlier to clean and set the things."

Arpad didn't say anything.

"It looks like you are quite devout and have been here all day. Most just come out with candles at night," Kaitlin said. She didn't inquire again why he was at this particular cemetery.

Soon the dusk gave into the night darkness where candles lit the entire cemetery, an upside down sky with amber stars. Families prayed, cried, missed and remembered.

Arpad found a nameless grave where no one was and lit a candle. He couldn't decide if his tears were for not remembering his deceased wife of ten years on this day or his resistance to praying for a new love, for he couldn't endure the pain of pleading to a God that may not exist.

Arpad never again went to Cafe V.

Love Is Not a True Word

I LIKED NARA WHEN SHE TOLD ME HER VERY FIRST STORY. Her English wasn't perfect but I understood her without fault because I loved her from the moment I heard her speak.

It was her shortest story: "My father named me after a Japanese city and he have never been to Japan. The town Nara is home to 1000 Sika deer."

I met Nara in New York City, a place quite far from the small farm town of El Chota in Ecuador where she was born.

The second story was about a Japanese myth which holds that the god Takemikazuchi came to Nara—the city—on a white deer, so the animals are considered messengers of God. Nara liked to joke—or I liked to think she was joking—that she too was a messenger of God.

The third story she told me was about a poppy, the beautiful flower, and how poppies have no scent.

We chuckled at that one but it was the kind of laughter that serves as a surrogate for tears. Neither one of us could proceed to cry from the cavernous source that was cognizant that our reality was no different than that of the poppies.

We cried later.

We told each other that we did. Somehow that felt like stating facts about something that happened to another.

Nara had a chypre scent. I wasn't really drawn to her fragrance as much as what I saw when I smelled her: varying colors of white, gray, dove gray, bronze, aubergine, and peacock green.

Nara bought me Ballentine's 30 year old scotch whiskey for my 50th birthday. I don't drink whiskey but she once told me a story about a man who wanted to attain wealth so he could bathe in a tub of whiskey. I had told her I had never had any.

I read Robert Frost's "Fire and Ice" in 8th grade. It was taught so we could learn similes and metaphors. I never understood why Robert Frost wanted the world to end in ice and, moreover, how a poet could become famous for writing such simple lines comparing and contrasting things.

I understood that poem for the first time when Nara told me a story about a group of scientists who said that the fate of the universe depends on which is stronger: the force of attraction or the force of repulsion. If the force of attraction is great then the universe will end in fire. If the force of repulsion is greater then it will end in ice.

I didn't understand the fate of Nara's universe.

One night after I made love to her, I told her we weren't like poppies.

"What are we like then?"

"Like daisies," I replied.

"I hate daisies. You can be a daisy but I am a pop-py. More useless than useful."

I didn't say anything that night unlike numerous other nights.

"Did you know the word "daisy" comes from the Anglo-Saxon *daeges eage* which means 'day's eye'."

I didn't know, and she knew I didn't know.

"Are you going to tell me a daisy story?" I tried to change her temperament.

"Fuck off."

The Nara I didn't understand stood up—naked—and I could see her body in the dark, an unfamiliar headless nymph.

Constant renewal.

After 20 years with Nara I didn't want to achieve much else but simply be. Happy, if possible.

Nara moved back to Guayaquil, Ecuador.

After I filed for divorce Nara didn't sign the pa-pers for two years. I didn't care if she ever signed them until I met someone else and needed her to sign them.

I went to Ecuador and she told me about her re-search on the region of Kansai, Japan. She had read quite a bit on it, how it encompassed Japan's third-largest city, Osaka and its former capitals, Kyoto and Nara, and Mount Koya.

"In Kansai's outlying cities you'll find the Japan of centuries-old shrines, temples, and pagodas, monks and geishas, tea ceremonies and long, languorous meals and many surprises in between," she said.

I listened without rushing her, partly because I didn't want to rile her and needed the divorce papers signed, but mostly because I missed her single sentence stories that never manifested longer than a paragraph.

Some—most—weren't even stories, just information she had collected, but the way she told them sounded like a story.

"Mount Koya is a beautiful little mountain town surrounded by eight peaks and saturated with towering moss-covered cedars. It is the home to the Shingon Buddhism sect and an area that, in many places, looks the same as it has for centuries," she said as she got up from the chair where she was sitting across from me at the table I had built for her.

"The sect began with Kukai—"

"Nara. Please," I cut her off.

She stared at me with eyes that flickered resentment. Or perhaps it was my reflection: I resented myself for at once stopping her and yet wanting her to continue.

She sat back down, heavy. She slowly reached for the pen and signed.

"Shingon means 'True Word'. The problem with our love—all love—is that love is not a true word unless you know what your shingon is," she said.

Some stories we understand better the more often we hear or read them. Other stories we can only understand the first time and thereafter we can never reach the same understanding.

Nara understood herself like a dream. Unfortunately.

Although I am the one who left her twenty years

ago, and have been remarried for the past 14 years to a woman who is constant, Nara is a dream I want to step back into regardless of whether or not it makes me happy.

Some are lucky. They are born knowing what would make them happy at seventy.

I am seventy and I now know: I want to hear stories.

Kinein

kinein, from the Greek, to move

All memories belong to a Love that can't be named.

OVIDIO OZSEB HERMANN, A RETIRED PHYSICS PRO-
FESSOR, WAS KNOWN FOR BICYCLING AROUND TOWN, a
small village town not distinct from neighboring towns
near Dorking, south of London in Surrey, England.

Ovidio often rode his bicycle on a small road
surrounded by rapeseed crops—a tall, rough weed-
like plant bursting with coarse yellow flowers—which
draped broadly and brightly across an always neutral
landscape. Some days he would stop by Ari's Shop, a
coffee shop that only served breakfast on Mondays.
Ari had decided this would be his contribution to the
small town—breakfast on Mondays—"because no
Monday was worth remembering, but a good breakfast could be."

"I can't remember what your house looks like,"
Ovidio said to Ari after he overheard Ari mention how
his wife wasn't happy with the pantry to another cus-
tomer.

"You have been there."

"I know but I can't recall it. Not one bit. Not the entrance. Not the rooms. None of it."

"Well, I suppose that's okay. I have, after all, moved three times in the last year and a half and you have been to the new place only once. And that too, a few months ago."

"No, no, it's not okay. Not at all. This is unsettling."

"Why don't you stop by sometime again and I am sure you will know you have been there before."

"It's not that, Ari. I just can't believe I have absolutely no recollection. I can't see it."

"It happens."

Ovidio took out money from his old leather wallet, which up until that point was unintentionally held tightly in his right hand to pay for his coffee which he liked without cream and with three sugars. Ari took the money and placed it in the cash register, then put the change—pennies—in a jar, upon receiving a nod from Ovidio.

Ovidio, before turning around so as to walk out of the small coffee shop, known as Shop, said, "It is strange. I am sure it will come to me."

It was only when Ovidio had stepped out of the Shop door that he suddenly recalled Ari's new home. Ovidio turned around and yelled, "I remember it! Ari! I remember it, Ari."

"See I told you! The gate around the big tree…the narrow entrance hallway…" Ari replied.

"Yeah, yeah. I know it now. Got all worried there for a second!"

"Worried? You don't got the age to worry about forgettin' stuff."

"I know, I know. Just strange that—"

"Strange to think a memory can disappear just like that. As if it never happened," said Ari.

Ovidio didn't reply but he was no longer smiling.

"What's the matter?" Ari inquired upon seeing Ovidio's face cave into grimness.

"I am not sure I know what your name means," Ovidio said out loud.

"Scalar?"

"Yes."

"I have told you what it means many times. You mean you don't understand what it means?" Scalar said in amusement.

Ovidio didn't respond.

"In physics, distance is a distinct quantity from either position or displacement. It is a scalar quantity, describing the length of the shortest path between two points along which the particle has traveled. A scalar is a simple physical quantity that is not changed by coordinate system rotations or translations or by space-time translations (in relativity).

The distance between two points in three-dimensional space is a scalar, but the direction from one of those points to the other is not, since describing a direction requires two physical quantities such as the angle on the horizontal plane and the angle away from that plane."

Ovidio didn't respond.

"Scalar is just a term capable of being represented by a point on a scale."

"Like love." Ovidio stated.

"Love can't be measured, Ovi, it is just a continuum."

"Where is it continuing to?"

"That's just it. It just continues, Ovi. Just goes on and on."

At this point Ovidio decided not to tell Scalar he loved her more than he had ever loved another woman.

"So you will love someone else after me and then after that someone else and just like rolling hills?"

Scalar remained quiet this time.

One can never forget the feeling a name induces. Scalar was such a name and it belonged to a woman who didn't believe in manifesting love in any form other than transiently loving.

Ovidio would race and move against winds, trains, thoughts, dreams, and memories, as he rode his bicycle around a golden town, never realizing it is movement, not memory that the heart desires.

Intuit

intuit: verb [trans.] *understand or work out by instinct.* ORIGIN late 18th cent. (in the sense [instruct, teach]): from Latin intuit- 'contemplated,' from the verb intueri, from in- 'upon' + tueri 'to look.'

THEY SAY SOMEWHERE NEAR INISHRUSH, IRELAND, THERE IS A NAMELESS, WHISTLE-STOP VILLAGE alongside Clady river, just upstream from the ford on Ford Road between Clady and Inishrush.

There you can find a man who tells you about horses' hooves and if you can understand him you understand everything about your life.

Aindriú Manus is his name and he is hard of hearing and even harder to decipher.

This is what he says:

My name is Aindriú Manus and I know horses. And that's about all I know. I suppose if you knew about horses you would say that is all anyone needs to know.

A horse's hoof is a structure evolved into a single weight-bearing digit of each of the four limbs. A single weight-bearing digit. You got a single weight-bearing digit? I can't even bear my weight on my two feet with ten digits. But you do got a single weight-bearing digit.

Ever heard of "no hoof, no horse"?

The horse hoof is not at all a rigid structure. It is elastic and flexible. Just squeezing the heels by hand will demonstrate that. No one knows that. Unless you know horses.

The hoof is made up by an outer part, the hoof capsule, and an inner, living part, containing soft tissues and bone. The walls are considered as a protective shield covering the sensitive internal hoof tissues as a structure devoted to dissipating the energy of concussion, and as a surface to provide grip on different terrains.

Since a single digit must bear the full proportion of the horse's weight that is borne by that limb, the hoof is of vital importance to the horse. The phrase "no hoof, no horse" underlines how much the health and the strength of the hoof is crucial for horse soundness.

I have told you the most important thing you need to know about horses and yourself.

That's all he says.

Memory of Silence

THE MEMORY OF SILENCE IS LOUD.

A distinct recollection I have, clear as the oxygen rich river, is that of an impromptu fishing trip in Montseny, Spain with my father. Montseny is a small village town near the Montseny Mountain Range west of the coastal hills of north of Barcelona, part of the Catalan Pre-Coastal Range. These are the highest mountains in the area south of the Pyrenees.

Down the valley, along the path of River Tordera, there are woodland walks that follow the river. The river flows into the sea between Blanes and Malgrat de Mar, collecting water from numerous torrents and brooks.

I am twelve and I feel the trees carry on a dialogue better than my father and I. But I am a twelve year-old boy then and I don't know whether fathers and sons should or shouldn't communicate any certain way with one another.

There we are, I can see us that day, sitting near the river, pants half folded up to our knees, chilled water despite the near perfect temperature around, in silence.

My father caught a fish that day. It was small. The eyes popped out and the fish's body was trembling to get out of the hook. The hook, stuck inside the mouth, looked the most unnatural. It wasn't my first time fishing but maybe it was the charm of Montseny, surrounded by a canvas of ethereal beauty, splendor of a hypnotic quietude I had never experienced before, but I didn't want to fish. There were things I wanted to say but didn't know how. Talking is taught. He was not a talker. I got up.

I continued to walk near River Tordera, floating in surreal colors that would leave a permanent imprint for future imaginings. I was surprised to see myself surrounded by lush green plants and these tiny dragonflies and damselflies.

The beguiling female damselflies known as Copper Demoiselles can be distinguished by a white spot on each of their four bronze wings. Their membranous wings of coppery silk are most enchanting. The large eyes, slender bodies, and small antennae made them so vulnerable yet inviolable. They danced undisturbed to the sounds of trees and glitter of sunbeams.

I grabbed one in my hand and looked at it up close and wondered if it could see me as clearly. I recall my father staring at me in my peripheral vision, standing against large stones that could never drown in the river, and within the next instant I crushed that demoiselle between by finger and thumb.

My father didn't say anything.

The walk back to where we were staying in Montseny was heavy. The barks on trees appeared rough, the noises from the fauna felt like sharp, knocking sounds instead of the harmony I had heard before.

Thirty years later, I too am a father now. I can't afford to take my two sons to magical places like Montseny. But I can tell them about a silence you don't want to remember.

Inspiratus

inspiration |inspəˈrā sh ən| noun c.1300, *"immediate influence of God or a god,"* especially that under which the holy books were written, from *Old French* inspiration, *from Latin* inspiratus: *"inspire, inflame, blow into," from* in-*"*in" + spirare *"to breathe."*

"in you everything sank!" —Pablo Neruda

MORE DANGEROUS THAN AN AFFAIR IS THE IDEA OF ONE. Affairs end; ideas live on once delivered to the imagination, Sogah.

I wake up in the middle of the night, Sogah— where is the middle when you never fall asleep? I dig through the wind's skin and scratch scratch scratch at nothing. I look for Vega, Lyra, Altair and million, million, stars, Sogah, to give me something, anything to ignite what was once there.

She wasn't like the others. She didn't have a provocative beautiful face—it was just a face. But her legs—like silverfish—offensively demanding of attention—had me. They were spindly, yet muscular. If observed with detachment they could have belonged to a young prepubescent boy fond of running around.

*

To understand desire—desire that rises like a torpedo within the pit of the groin, that vortex which can't be poked with fingertips—became an obsession. If it was merely lust it would have been satisfied with the object of desire; it was not lust to satisfy a physical urge. It was not to fulfill a void in my personal life. How many artists do you know who are still married to the same person who gave them two beautiful, intelligent teenage daughters? It was neither a yearning for a spiritual union, Sogah. So, help me understand, Sogah, what was it? Before her legs I hadn't picked up a paintbrush or pen or pencil like that to draw in how many years? Ten? Twelve? Her legs breathed life back to the artist that I once was. But she wasn't a muse, Sogah. I had continued to draw all these years without any recognition, awards, and with gallery exhibits not worthy of mentioning. You can't say I hadn't been inspired to create, Sogah. Most importantly, I continued to create before her.

The first pencil drawing I did of her—legs in a light twist dangling underneath a table, the evening sun highlighting the lines—was the first time I met her. It was a quick sketch, really, at *Le Vignette* coffee shop where I stop by on some Friday evenings. She was sitting there, stoic and steady, sipping her dark coffee, holding a blissful daze off into space. I realized I too wanted a glance into whatever space she was looking.

I showed her the sketch. She wasn't flattered like most women I had drawn previously. She said, "If I

didn't know any better, I would say you were in love."
I can't explain anything other than that, from thereon
I wanted to be with her—to create around her, with
her, of her. That night I went home and prepared to
expand the sketch of her legs, the coffee table, her legs,
and love of a fleeting moment into a 50 by 40 canvas.

I met her at *Le Vignette* again. And again. I made
love to her in my dreams. I made love to her when I
fixed breakfast for my wife and the two girls. I never
made love to her like I wanted.

One evening, the evening I most wanted to trace
my fingers alongside her legs, but instead stared at her
expressionless face, I told her something I had never
even told any of my art coaches. The Ones who had
tried their best to offer me positive platitudes, tech-
niques, and support to somehow thrust, nudge, and
coax me out of my creative slump.

I told her about Elizabeth Peyton.

She is an American painter who rose to popu-
larity in the mid-1990s, a contemporary artist best
known for stylized and idealized portraits. Her career
launched unexpectedly, a fact later endorsed by the art
market where the price of her works has steadily in-
creased. An oil on canvas representing John Lennon
was sold for a record $800,000 in 2006, Sogah! Works
by Elizabeth Peyton are now in the collections of the
Museum of Modern Art in New York and the Centre
Pompidou in Paris including other galleries.

Elizabeth Peyton's work is characterized by elon-
gated, slender figures with androgynous features. Her
work at times resembles fashion illustration. She has

indeed acknowledged the importance of photography as an inspiration source for her art. Her work is most often executed in oil paint, applied with washy glazes that are sometimes allowed or encouraged to drip. Several other works in colored pencil have also found notoriety, and recent work has included etchings.

I told her I wanted my art to be like Elizabeth Peyton: dripping everywhere.

She listened to me and then abruptly got up. She told me she didn't want to see me again. I panicked. I don't think a man can feel that sort of fright unless he loves, Sogah. So I touched her arm gently—for the first time—and told her, "I love you. You can't leave me."

"You don't love me. You are looking for God in your art. I am not art. I am not a messenger."

I told her she didn't understand love or art.

She got up and left. I watched her light, long legs carry her out the small door of *Le Vignette*.

I didn't sleep that night. I had dreams she would meet me again. She had to. She had been the answer all along. My wife didn't understand but there wasn't anything to hide. My wife and I had long negotiated what we were incapable of understanding about one another.

I went to *Le Vignette* next week but she wasn't there. She wasn't there the following week either. The third week I decided to stop by every day just in case she was now having coffee on a different evening than Fridays. I didn't see her any other day either.

I went back to my art coach. Now the coaching

wasn't even about my art but talking about *her*, the missing link.

I decided I was going to finish the 50 by 40 painting, now titled, "The Weight Bearing Structure." I cried some nights when I would take a break. I laughed at my genius other nights. One random Friday, when the painting was nearly finished, my daughter popped in the studio and told me the painting "was not sexy like legs are sexy" and that's why she liked it. I gave my daughter a big kiss on the forehead that very moment which caught us both by surprise and took the weekend off from painting and dreaming.

The Weight Bearing Structure.

I stopped going to *Le Vignette* for months. But Sogah...some afternoons have a way of carrying you back. I stopped by one such afternoon. She wasn't there. The barista asked me, "Are you the painter of 'Weight Bearing Structure'?" I told her I was.

She handed me a note. "This is from a woman. She said to give it to an artist named Julian. I saw your photo in the paper."

I knew who it was from. "When did she give this to you?"

"Two weeks ago."

When the painting was placed in the local exhibition.

The note read:

Julian
Mika Toimi Waltari was a Finnish writer, best

known for his best-selling novel The Egyptian. I share a quote from it: "I, Sinuhe, the son of Senmut and of his wife Kipa, write this. I do not write it to the glory of the gods in the land of Kem, for I am weary of gods, nor the glory of the Pharaohs, for I am weary of their deeds. I write neither from fear nor from any hope of the future but for myself alone. During my life I have seen, known, and lost too much to be the prey of vain dread; and as for the hope of immortality, I am as weary of that as I am of gods and kings. For my own sake only I write this; and herein I differ from all other writers, past and to come." Most have never heard of him. He changed my life. That is art. It transforms us the moment we read it, see it, or hear it. That is love too.

    -Rainy

Sogah, I love her.

There is no rehabilitation from an addiction to that kind of love that bursts open a light inside.

An affair with the imagination is a never-ending story and I just want another fix.

Help me, Sogah.

Ferraris and Lamborghinis

Children often grow up to forget that their parents—regardless of their intentions—were unreliable narrators for the facts of life.

AIX-EN-PROVENCE, A SMALL TOWN IN SOUTHERN FRANCE, WAS BUILT AROUND A DUAL IDENTITY: a town of water, a town of art. A visitor to France *felt* surprised to have *somehow ended up* in Aix, as the local residents often refer to it, even if he or she had *prepared* for a trip to ensure not missing out on this sun-drenched and easygoing hometown of Paul Cézanne.

Cours Mirabeau, one of the most famous streets in town, lined with green trees and cafés hosts a flea market on Sundays. On both sides of the road built in the 17th century, in the place of the former ramparts, the leading families of the nobility built elegant homes to show off their success, sometimes ostentatiously. With richly decorated frontages on the Cours side, and shared hidden gardens opening on to a parallel street, this architectural style created remarkable urban unity.

Composed of the Saint-Sauveur market town and the City of the Counts is the oldest part of the center of Aix known as Old Town. Some of the smaller streets in Old Town have kept their evocative names, such as the rue Esquicho-coudo, a narrow passage dating from the Middle Ages. Ruins of the old medieval ramparts may also be seen right at the top of the rue Gaston de Saporta. On Mondays the local residents take advantage of the missing crowd from Sundays.

It was on one such small street in Old Town where Lucas, who carried his mother's features well and at the age of nine had yet to show any similarities to the father, accompanied his father for a stroll on Monday afternoons.

Every Monday afternoon, without exception, Lucas and his father would come across the corner where a man in a blue hat, purple shirt, and pink socks sat, eating his meal laid out in several containers. The wall behind him held a collage of several murals. His bike was always parked next to him, as if ready for a painter to put it all on a canvas itself.

Lucas's father—not much for dialogue—would share his so called "facts of life" with Lucas during these Monday walks.

"Enzo Ferrari never intended to produce road cars when he formed Scuderia Ferrari," Luca's father told him one afternoon.

Lucas tried to listen as he contemplated why the man in the purple shirt always had, at least what appeared to him, a "picnic" out on the side of the street, and why his mother had said there were "things only his father could teach him" when she had sent him away to spend his summer with his father.

"Ferrari prepared, and successfully raced, various

drivers in Alfa Romeo cars until 1938, when he was hired by Alfa Romeo to head their motor racing department," the father stated.

He continued, "Alpha Romeo has competed successfully in many different categories of motorsport, including Grand Prix motor racing, Formula One, sports' car racing, touring car racing and rallies. They have competed both as a constructor and an engine supplier. The first racing car was made in 1913, three years after the foundation of A.L.F.A., the 40-60HP had 6 liter straight-4 engine. Alfa Romeo quickly gained a good name in motor sport and gave a sporty image to the whole marque."

Lucas wondered and shared aloud, "I am thinking this is not the same Romeo, like Juliet's Romeo?"

His father stopped in his tracks. He then turned around and looked at Lucas and said, "What good is your question? You think this would be the same Romeo as in the piss poor tale by some faggot that no one is even sure if he actually wrote it? Let me tell you a fact of life son, your questions determine answers which can determine your life. You got that?"

Lucas nodded.

They decided to sit on a bench from where they could still view the murals on the wall in front of which the man in the purple shirt enjoyed his meal, seated on the floor next to the wall.

"In 1941, Alfa Romeo was confiscated by the Fascist government of Benito Mussolini as part of the Axis Powers' war effort. Enzo Ferrari's division was small enough to be unaffected by this."

Lucas, uninterested, nodded. He couldn't help but indulge his fascination with the enriching colors splashed into images as a mural on the wall.

"What you get out of that?"

"I think the paintings are complex even if about simple things," Lucas replied.

"What?"

"You asked what I was thinking?"

"I asked you what you understood about Ferrari's division being too small!" his father exclaimed. And then laughed. The kind of laughter boys don't forget easily.

"I worry about you, you know," mumbled Lucas's father.

Two women passed by, one smiled at Lucas, the other didn't even notice him.

"And then came along Ferruccio Elio Arturo Lamborghini, the industrialist. In 1958 Lamborghini traveled to Maranello to buy a Ferrari 250GT, a two-seat coupé with a body designed by coachbuilder Pininfarina. He went on to own several more over the years, including a Scaglietti-designed 250 SWB Berlinetta and a 250GT 2+2 four-seater. Lamborghini thought Ferrari's cars were good, but too noisy and rough to be proper road cars, categorizing them as repurposed track cars with poorly-built interiors."

Lucas tried again. He listened intently: this had to be the information only his father could tell him as his mother had mentioned. He was overcome with anxiety however, given he had already forgotten who Alfa Romeo was.

"Who was Romeo again?" Lucas thought this was the right question.

"One year away and that mother of yours allowed you to turn into an idiot. Let me tell you something else Lucas, if you want to *succeed* at anything in life, you must remember no one is going to tell you the obvious twice. I didn't even tell you much about Alpha Romeo. My father made me research everything under the sun about Alpha Romeo when I was your age."

Lucas's father didn't mention, and Lucas would learn a few years later, prior to his mother marrying for the third time, that his father was raised in an orphanage.

The longer Lucas stared at the mural on the wall and the man—possibly homeless or in love with the moment—eating his lunch without once looking up, the less anxious he felt to remember his father's words.

"Lamborghini's mechanical know-how led him to enter the business of tractor manufacturing in 1948, when he founded Lamborghini Trattori. Isn't that something? Fact of life: you gotta make something of yourself, son."

Lucas contemplated if one needed crayons or colored pencils to draw the mural.

"After successfully modifying one of his personally-owned Ferrari 250GTs to outperform stock models, Lamborghini gained the impetus to pursue an automobile manufacturing venture of his own, aiming to create the perfect touring car that he felt no one could build for him."

Lucas didn't know then that this very moment

would mark the beginning of his fascination and repulsion to art.

"Lamborghini found that Ferrari's cars were
equipped with inferior clutches, and required continu-
ous trips for rebuilds. Lamborghini brought his mis-
givings to Enzo Ferrari's attention, but was dismissed
by the notoriously pride-filled Modenan—the capital
of engines."

"Now. Let's get you some dinner," Lucas's father
said cheerily. They got up from the bench to walk away
from the wall with the mural and the man in the purple shirt. Lucas turned around to look at the mural one
more time. His father noticed and commented, "Oh
that—don't even bother looking at it. Tomorrow I am
going to take you to a real art museum." And he laid
his hand over his son's shoulder—removing it quickly—and continued about the craft of a good racecar.

Lucas would barely remember this afternoon
when he was twenty-five years old only to dismiss
his entire childhood with his father as a counterfeit
memory; a father, he concluded, who knew only about
Ferraris and Lamborghinis, and nothing about art, history, or the world.

*Children recall their past—regardless of the accuracy—
as an equally unreliable narrative.*

Infinity's Muse

"The minute I heard my first love story I started looking for you, not knowing how blind that was. Lovers don't finally meet somewhere. They're in each other all along."
—Rumi

"MUCH EASIER TO DRAW OR PAINT THAN WRITE, KRISTO."

"Here you go again. Putting my art down."

"I am not putting your art down—I am trying to bring your attention outside of your self-absorbed-narcissistic-selfish-self to what I do is hard—hard work."

"I never said you didn't work hard, Lidia"

"You don't even listen! That is how full of yourself you are. I didn't say work hard but how much *harder* writing is *than* dabbing strokes—meaningless fucking strokes which turn into a *'tender, new sensation of the lost art of Art.'*"

"Oh God. Please tell me this is not about the painting 'Fractal.' That was three years ago, Lidia. I am tired of going through this every few months!"

"Three years ago that changed our lives."

"That is art: it takes a life of its own."

"Yeah and she lived—and probably *still* lives—in your head in order to take life into that form."

"There is no *she*, Lidia. How many times—"

"Of course there is! 'Fractal' *is* she. Every review even said so— *'alchemy possible when an object moves even the muse'* —And even everything *after* 'Fractal' has smudges of her."

"Reviewers review artwork however they want! I have no control over that Lidia!"

"Yes you do! You could have said *something* in *any* of the interviews—any—Kristo!" Lidia yelled on the verge of an hysterical outburst.

She walked over to the coffee table, knocking over some cushions from the edge of their oversized sofa, picked up the latest edition of *Art in America* magazine, and tried opening to her husband's latest interview. Her frenzy made her unsuccessful and so she tossed the magazine on the floor.

"I don't need to find it. You know what you said."

Only a few are lucky enough to marry their muse, a muse they love a lifetime, Kristo had quipped during the interview and then had added, *This was just right out of a memory I don't recall but dreamt again and again.*

"Nothing ever happened with Sophia. We know this. You know this. The so called 'evidence' you found even spells it out: *nothing ever happened* with Sophia. She was just a stranger you run into a few times. And then they are gone. She wasn't even a fan!"

"What else you got before 'Fractal' then, huh?" screamed Lidia.

"I've got lots before. It's not about "got" when you create. You should know this. You write for Christ's sake!"

"I don't believe in Christ."

"Well, then for f—", Kristo didn't finish, for Lidia had already left their living room stuffed with family photographs, books, art magazines, and the fine line between responsibility and love.

All affairs—those imagined and real—find their beginning in the way someone says a name.

"No one calls me Kristo."

"Would you rather I call you Kris?"

"I like how you say my name. I like that you call me Kristo,"

Sophia smiled. "I like your name because I can turn it into an infinity symbol," Kristo told her, amused.

"You can't turn my *entire* name into it. Just the letter 'S'."

"I love your name, Sophia. Sophia. It sounds like someone's wife's name. Hopefully my future wife."

"You already have a wife, Kristo."

Kristo ignored Sophia's last comment.

"I love saying your name. So-phi-ah: a pastel whisper rolls and lingers to be longed for.

"Is your wife an artist too?"

"No. She is artistic but not quite an artist."

"There is a difference?"

"Yes. Sure."

"What is it?"

"A difference between lines, forms, and shapes.

Both perceive the lines and shapes similarly through the eyes but for one they eventually bend and contort by the time they reach *here*," Kristo took Sophia's hand which he wanted to kiss but didn't and placed it on his heart, "and what comes out is not exactly of your own volition."

"Like you are possessed?"

"Yes."

Kristo took in Sophia's disturbed countenance.

"I am only possessed by you, Sophia."

"I came to give you something. Read it after I leave," Sophia said and got up to leave Kristo along with her unfinished coca-cola drink diluted by ice cubes.

Kristo opened the card. It read: *"Dear K. It matters not if I say I love you because you already know I do. However, you are wrong, love is not like infinity, it is like gravity."* And then a quote by the poet Rumi printed in the middle of the card, *"There are lovers content with longing. I'm not one of them."* Then Sophia's handwriting continued, *"Please don't contact me again. We didn't have a beginning and I want to keep it that way. Let's sublimate and forge something another way. Hope you understand."* She had signed the card with her first initial "S," as a vertical infinity symbol.

The painting titled "Fractal" sat in a small gallery, Luca Fine Art Gallery, in Morhall for three months without anyone noticing it. The art gallery was in the middle of hilly Bright Pine Street, the elevation just enough so as to make parallel parking challenging on both sides of the street, but the green drenched trees in the summertime made up for parking provocations. And then, just like it sometimes is, the reviews of "Fractal" provided a vivacity for Kristo's art, which he had been longing for unconsciously. The arts section of the local newspaper reviewed it as *"tender, new sensation of the lost art of Art"* and in the next few weeks Kristo found himself part of an international commotion he had never desired as an artist. "Fractal" was soon showcased at various galleries through different cities.

It was an acrylic piece of an ordinary face sprawled on a large canvas but it did hypnotize, even if momentarily. It was going to stay and maybe even pass the test of time.

Fractal is a curve or geometric figure, each part of which has the same statistical character as the whole. It can be magnified indefinitely without losing structure and becoming smooth. Fractals are good at describing partly random or chaotic phenomena such as crystal growth, fluid turbulence, and galaxy formation.

At the foothill, Bright Pine Street curved onto another street which led to an abandoned railway station. Although the area was deserted during the day, the waiting area near the tracks hardly felt empty at night given it was very well-lit.

Kristo learned astronomy from his late grandfather who had once worked in an observatory. "See all those books about stars? All that knowledge in them is no good unless you can tell some woman about them," his grandfather had once told him as he pointed Ursa Major to Kristo's nine year-old fascination.

It was also Kristo's grandfather who told him the story of the abandoned railway station. If a person walked up to and sat near the railway at the deepest hour of the night, memories and dreams packed within, he might see a train flash by that decides he is the last passenger it forgot to take along. And although you didn't get on board literally, it rushed along, a quicksilver flash, suspending all thoughts so you could see a vision.

With every breath Kristo drew Sophia closer. The only form of communication that doesn't have a limit consumed their every nerve. Kristo had drawn her several times before, mostly in his dreams, but now he could trace each curve and crevice beyond the stroke of the brush. Sophia, saturated in meteoric motion, became a fishnet for understanding that defied articulation. He loved that she liked his shoulders. Scanning each others' thoughts simultaneously dipped them into an unexpected laughter: ecstasy borne out of the knowledge of being adored for exactly the secret blueprint held inside one's head for what a beloved should notice—shoulders, lines on a lip, long fingers, and even something like handwriting...

Kristo began working on Fractal soon after. The months that followed, every night, Kristo waited as the last passenger near the railway track, to draw Sophia closer, so he could finish Fractal. But Sophia continued to come to him long after Fractal was finished as long as he was not afraid to be the last passenger.

While Sleeping

*Losing too is still ours; and even forgetting still has a
shape in the kingdom of transformation.*
—Rilke

Faizel met Daisy, a woman who would eventually agree to marry him, on the train from Rome to La Spezia. Daisy was headed to Cinque Terre, located off the picturesque western Italian Rivera near La Spezia, and Faizel decided to join her.

He mistook her traveling alone through Italy for passion to explore, whereas Daisy had a checklist of things to do before getting married one day soon. Through pure coincidence, which Faizel didn't believe in, Daisy was staying in the first village town, Monterossa, one of the five towns which comprised Cinque Terre, a town he wished to see during his stay with friends in La Spezia.

Daisy, as he would later learn, was a name she had chosen for herself. She had a domineering air and a mouth that held a life of its own. At times her mouth coordinated well with the sentiments reflected in her eyes; other times, most of the time, the mouth was aloof and projected a huge, hallow grin. But her mouth was an artist's dream or at least the artist Faizel was at that age where you believe a spark of love in Italy can carry a relationship through a lifetime.

"I want you to be like this simple silver band I wear—*right here*—on my middle finger. I know it won't slip off no matter which ocean I go under," Daisy told Faizel while sitting as still as she could so he could finish her sketch.

"You don't even like oceans, so you will never go under," Faizel replied without looking up from the drawing.

They had, as new lovers still unscathed from too many relationships, shared in the forty-eight hours of knowing one another what they thought created intimacy: favorite colors to cities in Italy, to fears, dreams, goals, and a few heartbreaks from the past.

"That looks ugly. You think I am ugly?" Daisy said after she took a look at the sketch.

"You think it's ugly? You don't like it?"

"It's not me. I don't look like that."

"You are beautiful. Your mouth is beautiful and—" Faizel paused, "—I am sorry you don't like it."

"Art makes things more beautiful than they are. Look at Italy!" Daisy exclaimed trying to hold back tears unsuccessfully.

"No, no, no.....art...it brings to light what we forget is beautiful."

"Well, this—this right here—is neither. It's simply distorted. My mouth is not that big."

Although they didn't speak for the rest of the afternoon, after dinner they reconciled while laying on the pensione's balcony. They moved the thin foam mattress from the bed inside to the balcony floor so as to fall asleep under a sky that Faizel told Daisy he wished to paint one day, a sky that held nothing extraordinary for her. Faizel traced her scars that couldn't be seen, only felt, and Daisy thought it was satisfactory sex. Faizel decided he was in love with her and her uncomplicated world.

Two years later, he asked Daisy to marry him when she came to visit him in Chicago from Florida. "You give me stability that I have been unable to carve for myself. Will you marry me?"

He threw away an old memento a week before proposing to Daisy. He had never quite held on to it yet never tossed it either. The memento was a note written to him from a woman he thought he had loved: *the gold specks in your green-stained eyes linger on my bronze skin long after you have kissed every inch.*

That same night, a week before proposing, Faizel distinctly recalled his uncle's decision to take on a life-long mistress. "I married your auntie for the man I thought I ought to be. She is a good woman with ugly calves. Saleen, on the other hand, brings out the man I want to be. For remember this, Faiz, we are all two people, and you will decide which person you like being more."

It would take many years into his own marriage for Faizel to put together that his uncle, an inadequate father-figure, neither became the man he wanted to be with Saleen nor what he thought he ought to be with his wife.

Thirty-six years with Daisy, every night, he would meet the mirror that falls like a screen before one's eyes, reflecting, another self, another life. *We are all more than one self, after all,* he could hear his Nana— his uncle's wife—say before the mirror would retract and his heavy eyelids created the pathway to pass through another night.

There are dissolutions to relationships that do not necessitate a separating. They persist by filling space with what once was, even if it was never really there.

Engram

|'engram| noun *a hypothetical permanent change in the brain accounting for the existence of memory; a memory trace.*

THE DARKNESS BELONGS TO NO ONE BETWEEN THE HOURS OF THREE AND FOUR. It is a suspension of theories, feelings, and conclusions that adhere neither to the night nor to the day. It is a podium wreathed with dreams, memories, and thoughts that are not quite yours to claim. What can't be deciphered in those hours is invented for coherence.

Winds carry stories in them.

Some nights I like to think the stories in the wind that come with the darkness belong to me. I wish all stories were love stories. I don't know why I wish this since most love stories never manifest the way anyone wants, and if they do it is because we don't know the whole story, only clinging to those parts of a story we do know.

The benevolent fog eases the darkness. The thin cloud of mist is an adhesive around the skin, an opaque cool that soothes the dry surface of existence. Fog differs from clouds only in that fog touches the surface of the Earth. My mother used to say foggy mornings meant the earth had exhaled deeply. She liked salty sea air dabbled in her foggy mornings. At night the fog is different.

Fidda Miroslav, my mother, kept my father's name even though no one knows where he went after I turned seven. She neither filed for divorce nor did she allow others to assert that he was dead. He was just *away*.

In sixth grade Mrs. Lucas, my science teacher, called my mother for a conference to discuss that I might possibly have Asperger's Syndrome, a form of high-functioning autism. Apparently whether Asperger's Syndrome is it's own disorder or part of a spectrum of autism is disputed nowadays. Anyway, unlike most mothers, my mother neither panicked nor argued with Mrs. Lucas. She politely listened and then replied, "He is not autistic; he is just eccentrically *ar*tistic." My mother never attended another conference with Mrs. Lucas after that despite the teacher's many attempts throughout the year.

Mrs. Lucas—a woman whose hair always smelled like fried bacon—was alerted to my "artistic" nature when she learned of my obsession with the "twin paradox." In physics the twin paradox is a thought experiment in special relativity in which a twin makes a journey into space in a high-speed rocket and returns home to find he has aged less than his identical twin who stayed on Earth. This led to intense research on thought experiments, where given the structure of the proposed experiment, it may or may not be possible to actually perform the experiment, which further resulted in reading book after book on the special theory of relativity and time dilation. The question of whether something happening at one location is in fact happening simultaneously with something happening elsewhere became the focal point of all my observations.

My mother died when I was still in high school. I didn't cry even though, being her only son, I missed her terribly. I knew then no one would understand me like she had. It wasn't until I graduated from college with honors in Physics that I cried. After the night I cried, which seemed like the longest night, I never again considered whether I had Asperger's Syndrome.

My son, Ingram, tells me they are right: I have early signs of dementia. They have got some fancy name for it now, which I forget. The difference between typical age-related change and my memory loss is that those who have the "typical" can remember what they forget within some acceptable time frame.

Signs of my dementia include memory loss that disrupt daily life: forgetting recently learned information, important dates or events, and asking for the same information over and over; or trouble following a familiar recipe or keeping track of monthly bills; losing track of dates, seasons and passages of time; trouble understanding something if it is not happening immediately; forgetting where one is or how he or she got there; and in terms of perception, passing a mirror and thinking someone else is in the room.

I am not going to lie; I do become confused, suspicious, depressed, fearful or anxious. I do. But I was always sensitive. I think it is good to be sensitive.

Last night Ingram told me about his "friend" Lucielle. I thought he wanted to talk about a new woman given he has been divorced for two years now. But instead, he told me how Lucielle is considering assisted suicide for her mother who is very ill with terminal cancer and endures anguishing chronic pain where she wails through the night. Lucielle lost her job because she had to take care of her mother and couldn't afford a nurse or a nursing home.

I asked Ingram if he wanted to kill me. I'm not sure why, but that shocked him.

He left me alone at the dinner table with left-over pot roast that Lucielle had cooked two nights ago. No different than how his mother had walked away fifteen years ago, except she left for good. No different than his wife who cried during their last dinner together because she couldn't continue taking care of him and me. I can't help thinking that these last dinners happen elsewhere simultaneously except people don't leave but they choose to stay instead.

Ingram says the grandchildren find it frustrating that I stop in the middle of a conversation and sometimes repeat myself or struggle with vocabulary or call things by the wrong name. Doesn't everyone?

Tomorrow I meet with Ingram and an attorney to draft my will. If my condition worsens I don't want Ingram to suffer along with me and I don't want to continue like they say. Besides, without remembering, I don't know how I would make it through the dark

hours of the fog that no one can own.
    Alzheimer's. That's the fancy name for it.

The False Door

Around the bend of Fort Street is a local dive bar which is easy to miss even if you are walking. The "NO Smoking Inside" metal sign, which reads "Smoking Inside" because the "N" and "O" faded off too long ago for Nusrat, the owner, to recall fixing it, gave the dive bar its name: "O Smoking." Inside, a fog of stale smoke mixed with recent exhales welcomes you. Winter nights are even worse. The eye-inflaming smoke is even thicker since the tabagie refuse to huddle outside to light their cigarettes.

Usually the workers from the factory plants in the surrounding area stop by after their shifts for a couple of beers. None of them mind when the beers aren't as chilled as the televised advertisements make them appear. However, every once in awhile, people from a town fifteen miles north or a town twenty miles south stop by on the weekends.

Emerald Reeves decided to stop by "O Smoking" on an evening that was on the lookout for a rainy night. She was on her way home further south right after work up north. She had stopped at a nearby gas station which had one pump unit to buy a pack of cigarettes. She became nostalgic for Paris all of a sudden where she could buy one cigarette from a pass-erby instead of a whole pack at a store. But that was long ago. Now that she was no longer pregnant she could smoke even though she was not a smoker. After her first cigarette in over a decade she felt hungry. She asked the young man behind the counter if there was a diner within the unfrequented area. He informed her there wasn't one but that there used to be one next to the dive bar. Emerald became aware of her urge to touch the man's lightless eyes. *Did her eyes appear simi-larly to him?* She couldn't decide. He wasn't sure if they served food at "O Smoking" he told Emerald, as she walked out to her car.

She stepped inside "O Smoking" and trudged past a few glances towards her—more because she was a new face and less because she was a decent looking woman in her late 30's—and sat on one of the stools at the bar. Nusrat was bar-tending that night. She was relieved and saddened to be left alone.

After an hour Nusrat finally said to her, "If you gonna keep drunken' like that who's gonna drive you home?"

Emerald didn't respond other than, "I am taking it easy. Don't worry."

The kitchen, which served only hot dog and fries, was closed because Baru, who ran it, had called in sick. A few minutes later she found herself inside the smallest restroom, even for a dive bar, with two toilet stalls, one of which worked. She took her pro-jectile vomiting as a sign that indeed, God wanted her to drive home safely. Exhausted, she sat on the dirty floor, with her back against the toilet. She tilted her head to put the wooden stall door in perspective. *Why didn't the door touch all the way to the floor?* She almost giggled at the thought that maybe these doors were made this way intentionally for occasions like these, so that she and others in her predicament could crawl out from underneath them when they couldn't stand up. Emerald decided to sit there just a little longer and stare at the montage of scribbled notes on the wall: *Call Tina for a good time 312-6695. Star and Rody forever* inside a drawing of a wobbly lined heart. She couldn't make out if it was Rody or Rudy. She gleaned over many other notes with names, some followed by numbers.

Emerald decided to take out her black pen—the one that was part of "office property that no one should take out of the office" but everyone did—and wrote a line from the poet Rilke: *How can I keep my soul in me, so that it doesn't touch your soul? How can I raise it high enough, past you, to other things?* And then added, *Call Emery if you have a soul* followed by her number.

She drove into the light rain without saying good-bye to Nusrat. Once home she told her husband she didn't want to speak to him or sleep next to him and never wanted to have children with him.

One year later Emerald received a call from a man who said he was calling from a phone booth near "O Smoking."

"Is this Emery?" he asked.

"Are you there?" he said gently since there was no

response.

Did this really happen? Did people actually call people whose numbers they found in bathroom stalls? Emerald was at a loss for words.

"Hello?" he spoke into the phone.

"Yes. I am. I am here."

"Hi. Is this an okay time to call Emery?"

"Yes. Emerald. All who called me Emery are long gone," she replied, unsure why she had added the last bit of information.

There was silence but the awkwardness had already passed. She was too embarrassed to inquire how he had come upon her number in a woman's bathroom stall. Moreover, her body was repulsed at reliving that day and evening. He too was glad she didn't.

For the next month, every Tuesday night, Sefu called Emery from a phone booth near the factory where he worked during the day. Sefu was handsome but didn't appear interesting and for a man, unlike a woman, that equated to no allure for the opposite sex.

Once during their phone conversation he told her about Ka, the Egyptian concept of spiritual essence, that which distinguishes between a living and a dead person, with death occurring when the *ka* leaves the body. Sometimes the ka was slow to leave the physical realm.

Another time, Sefu told Emerald about the False Door. It was a wooden architectural element inside Ancient Egyptian tombs in front of which funerary offerings were usually placed. A false door is usually carved from a single block of stone or plank of wood, and it was not meant to function as a normal door. Located in the center of the door is a flat panel, or niche, around which several pairs of doorjambs are arranged—some convey the illusion of depth and a series of frames, a foyer, or a passageway.

"The False Door served as a link between the living and the dead," Sefu added.

"How old are you?" Emerald asked.

"What? What does that have to do with anything?"

"I want to know how old you are, Sefu."

"One," he replied and giggled.

"Don't ever call me again."

"What?"

"I don't want to hear from you again." Emerald hung up the phone. When her husband came home from work she finally told him they could have had a child and he would have been one year old. She just never wanted to have his children.

Sefu understood nights as a segue between the now and then. He didn't understand why he was called to assist others release the *ka*.

"To and Fro"

<small>CATS ARE PARTICULAR ABOUT WHERE THEY SIT.</small>

Two cats named To and Fro by their rather distrait owner, often sat atop a credenza—a piece of furniture that became very fashionable during the second half of the 19th century—looking out the window. This credenza had small pieces of variously colored polished wood. The surface felt cool and clean underneath their paws.

Originally in Italian the name credenza meant belief. This was because in the 16th century the act of credenza was the tasting of food and drinks by a servant for a lord or for another important person. By tasting it they made sure the food was not poisoned. The name passed then to the room where the act took place, then to the furniture.

No one plans on being alone at fifty years old.

"Oh there you go again with that thought!" said To.

"Just let me think what I want to think," retorted Fro.

"You forget I can hear your thoughts," To responded.

"You forget I can hear yours too but do you hear me interrupting?"

"Well, frankly, if they are the same ones it gets pretty boring to hear them. Don't you get bored thinking the same thoughts?"

Fro didn't care to reply.

The cats sat there and saw a young man park his bicycle against the wall to meet a woman who was very much in love with him. He had been visiting her every night for the last month. Sometimes they would take a stroll along the street where she lived and other times he would just sit on her front doorstep and talk with her.

"The boy knows how to flatter her," said To.

"She is self-conscious about her skin, hair color, posture and weight," replied Fro.

"She is not obese. You make her sound obese. She is in pretty good shape for her age," exclaimed To.

"*You* are obese," snapped Fro.

"It's rude to tell a cat it is fat."

"Not if you are a cat yourself," noted Fro.

"Well, no exercise coupled with her thyroid issues and metabolism slowing down with age, I say she is doing well."

But the boy's compliments are sincere despite his uncanny ability to decipher what needs to be said.

"Can you be quiet!" To screamed.

"I wasn't thinking anything! I said that out loud!"

To was certain Fro had said that in his own head but decided not to engage with him.

Most of us are living to die yet are afraid of death.

"Don't," Fro said quickly before To could say anything, "Just let me be." His thoughts heavy and beyond him.

In between we catch glimpses of whatever we wanted this life to be but deemed it incapable of being. How could living how you wanted really be that simple?

"There they go…off into the thin night to kitten around," whispered To.

Pansy shifted to the other side where she could see her two cats To and Fro. She scanned her living room from the sofa: a pile of plastic bottles that needed to be recycled (she didn't care to count how many), unfolded laundry on one brown sofa chair with a small hole in the slipcover, sealed letters blended with opened unsolicited advertising mail from months ago, the lamp that needed a new light bulb which she hadn't bought in weeks because light came through the street lamp outside.

The man and woman, not quite in their mid-twenties, walked past the window and waved at To and Fro. The girl commented how she loved these two cats that sat there every night, never to be seen during the day. The boy added they made for a perfect window dressing. They couldn't help but wonder what radiated inside, too young to know that houses never looked the same from inside as they did from the outside.

Pansy dismissed the younger woman, her neighbor, as a wild fauna of a society at large that never understood the demands that a real life beckons: bills, skills, social and marital engagements, a long marriage, rearing children, surviving the physical signs and pains of aging. Essentially, as far as Pansy was concerned, the young woman knew nothing about living.

Armageddon is now, thought Fro.

But so are we, To thought louder, *there is a choice*.

Upon hearing To's thought, Fro replied, "There isn't a choice."

Pansy thought of the story of the Egyptian goddess of the night known as Nut. Her father had told her this story when she was little to comfort Pansy when she didn't want to sleep alone. Tefnut, the goddess of moisture, mated with Shu, the god of air, to give birth to Sky, known as goddess Nut, the goddess of nighttime sky. Goddess Nut was known as the barrier separating the forces of chaos from the ordered cosmos of the world. Her father had told Pansy that some people belonged to the night to continue working for Goddess Nut.

Pansy didn't mind being alone and reminded herself of that every morning. She just wished she didn't have to hear her cats' thoughts when she couldn't sleep.

Reflection of Love

Some loves take the form of binary stars. The double stars orbit a common center of mass and often appear as a single visual or telescopic object when they actually are not.

BLAIZE DIDN'T UNDERSTAND SPIRITUALITY IN ANY FORM—with or without religion. But he understood something he could never quite articulate, even to himself, when he met Afet for the first time.

"No one names their child Blaize in this day and age."

"Why-a?" Blaize asked, drawing Afet closer to him as they stood underneath the rotunda of the classicist building.

Afet was enamored with, and would continue to desire, the way Blaize's neck muscles stretched along his pronounced collarbones. And the way he would say why, stressing an unnecessary but welcome "a" sound at the end.

"I don't know. Do you know anyone besides Blaise Pascal named Blaise? And that too with a zed."

"I like how you are learning my culture. Zed and not Z."

"Oh please! It is not your culture. Over half the world pronounces the alphabet zed and not z."

He kissed her. Their first kiss.

They had met two days ago in a park around the same rotunda beneath which they were now standing. Sometimes he wondered whether his only knack was for spotting tourists. But Afet had made it easier than usual—she had inquired about a street nearby that every local knew. He had convinced her to see him the next day for dinner. He desired her immediately and reluctantly and therefore knew his feelings were unusual.

"You kiss nice," Afet said and looked up at him with her blithe grin.

The silence was saturated with possibilities that exist between a man and a woman.

Blaize knew they had no future. He had never been able to take on the responsibilities that came with love.

The air smelt of rotten eggs due to the high concentration of sulfur coming from the hot running water around the rotunda.

"You said at dinner last night you wanted to tell me a story," Afet reminded him.

"Come. Let's walk to the park and I will tell you," Blaize replied. He gently held her hand—peculiarly small—and guided her to the park.

"Tell me," she said. This is when Blaize first became aware that he liked the sound of her voice; contrarily, it was tranquil when she was eager.

Blaize began, "Saint Blaise was a physician and bishop of Sebastea, Armenia, now modern Turkey. According to his Acta Sanctorum—"

"What's that?" Afet interrupted.

"What's what?"

"Acta–?"

"Acta Sanctorum is, you know, like an encyclopedia of the Saints."

"Oh. I didn't know," she replied, and realized she wanted him to infiltrate her with everything he knew.

"According to Saint Blaise's Acta Sanctorum he was endowed with miraculous healing power and is the patron who cured throat illnesses and even healed animals." Blaize said quietly.

They were now in the dark park, underneath a starless night.

"That's it? That's your story? I can't believe I believed you during dinner!" Afet exclaimed in that calm voice of hers, a puff of exasperation without an exclamation.

At dinner the night before, Blaize had told her he wanted to share a story that could only be told in the night. He had also told her he wanted to spend the rest of his life with her. Afet wanted to not believe him and then dismissed his sentiments as lust.

The rotunda was slightly visible from where they now stood in the park. The cool grass welcomed their walk.

Blaize kissed her again. And again. Her hands awakened into his. Slowly the hungry union reached a crescendo beyond the deep chasm of an ethereal enigma that encompasses human frailty and ecstasy.

"Now I know why you tell stories in the dark,"

Afet said jokingly and got up from the ground to fix her skirt.

"Sometimes we love so deeply that it remains close to us eternally, orbiting all other loves, yet that is the one love we can never touch again," Blaize said.

"Do you love me?" Afet asked him. Her voice had changed. She wanted this to last beyond an eager desire to make a moment longer than its expiration.

Blaize didn't answer her that night, nor any other night that she was still a tourist in his town.

Five years later when Blaize saw Afet again, for the fourth and last time, he shared that he loved her. He recalled her linen turquoise scarf immediately. It was the same one she had worn the night they were together in the park near the rotunda, wrapped loosely around her long neck. They sat across from each other and caressed the memory of a night that was full of possibilities, a night which could have held a canopy of stars, despite the missing magic. That was also the night Blaize began to preserve the sound of her voice for days to follow. Afet told him this was not a movie and he didn't know what love was.

Afet did't cry when she left him but she accepted that she had never stopped wanting that kind of love.

If, on the contrary, two stars should really be situated very near each other, and at the same time so far insulated as not to be materially affected by the attractions of neighboring stars, they will then compose a separate system, and remain united by the bond of their own mutual gravitation towards each other. This should be called a real double star; and any two stars that are thus mutually connected, form the binary sidereal system.

Apnea

THEY SAY I LURK AROUND GRAVES.

The wife told me to get checked out by them mental technicians. She didn't speak to me the rest of dinner last week after I called a head doctor a "mental technician." I think that is a better term, no? Not *all* my marbles are loose up there. Maybe I need a little tweaking and that's all. Doesn't everyone? The wife tried to convince me that I have sleep apnea and that's why I can't sleep. But I know her. Men know their women. Some of us just don't know what to do with what we know. I know that was her way of making me go get checked up.

Yesterday I got back home around 5:30 a.m. The sun had barely started making its way when I stepped inside to find her sitting on the sofa I had bought five years ago, the sofa she doesn't like. I asked her if she was getting ready for work. She responded, angry at me, "5:30 a.m. Why would I get ready at 5:30 in the morning? And does it look like I am getting ready for work?"

"I thought today you had the morning shift," I had replied. I was sincerely confused.

I told her I was sorry and that I had gone on a

walk. Same as night before. And the night before that. And the week before that. And the month before that. And the months before that. She told me–again– "You need to get help. I get sick worrying about you when you go walking out in the middle of the night."

I don't like when she cries but I never know what to tell her when she does. Our son, who is seven, walked down the stairs, not knowing what to ask us. Suddenly I couldn't recall what day it was. She told him to go back to bed but Jacob just stood there. So I walked over to him and ran my right hand over his matted hair.

I want to know what kind of a man he is going to grow up to be. I want to know what can I do: can I even do anything? Jacob turned around and went back up stairs.

"What the fuck do you do out there?" she asked me like she had many times before.

"Nothing. I just walk, Marcy."

"They said that you go—someone said—Mr. Perry told Martha's husband that he saw you in the cemetery."

"Yes. I told you that last week. I got sick of goin' to the park."

"It's *not* normal," Marcy said. And repeated, "Why don't you want to get help?"

"What for? I am back am I not? I go to work. I don't need as much sleep as some that's all," I told her like I had many times before.

"Why can't you go on these walks in the day?"

I can't think during the day I wanted to tell her.

The darkness at night terrorizes me yet guards me.

"Mr. Naidoo, you know the Indian nurse I told you about? Who just started working over time? Told me his wife doesn't sleep much since–since–they lost their baby."

Marcy had had a miscarriage two years ago. I saw it as a blessing in disguise. I thought we both had always wanted only one child. Jacob was great. After that we had decided Jacob was enough.

"Well, she should take some medicines for that or go see a head doc," I told her. I didn't say mental technician.

I walked upstairs to sleep for a few hours.

A different fragment from the same dream was tossed my way and would make its way into the night.

The earth grated her bare feet as she ran, not desirous of any particular destination. Dry breaths pumped out of her cold lungs. She didn't mind the rush from running on the crusty ground that perforated the soles of her feet. She ran into and out of branches that hung low from the jacaranda trees. Purple has an image-smell; it just smells like something. She ran through magenta and violet leaves vaporizing an unspecified burnt scent. The deep plum shades added another layer to the heavy darkness of the night in spite of the plump moon.

Her thoughts, rapid contractions, reverberated faster than the branches grazing her as she ran through them.

I love you…I heard myself say.

First contraction felt deeper than any cramping she had endured before.

*you make me a better man…*I heard myself say.

Second contraction pounded her and she could see the pain, a bulldozer hammering through her.

*we have a choice…*I hear a voice say.

Third.

And when she could no longer contain the pain shooting through her groin and her lower stomach, she collapsed, digging her hands through the solid earth, feeling her insides begin to invert. She coiled herself in the fetal position, face on the ground, to feel the earth exhale.

She tried to pull herself by a branch that hung lowest, a friend's hand to lift her body, but it cracked without much noise despite the silence of the dark.

She rolled over and propped her head against a bunch of bushes. The violet leaves swayed to make room for her to glimpse the fat moon. She saw red rocks in the moon instead of the usual grey blotches. The wind rustled the jacaranda leaves.

I sometimes walk at night and think of the son I could have had with Maria. She said it was her choice. I think I could have stopped her. I feel her choice like she made it last night and ran out. I just want her to know I felt everything with her. The graves understand.

Some memories eclipse and stretch the night into a field where we stay until the sun saves us.

The Love of Your Life

*"Night returns with armful of stars…Already a
thin light is aiming through the night for any heart. "*
—Kobus Moolman

THERE IS A MAN FROM SOUTH AFRICA THAT ROAMS
THE SHORELINES AROUND THE GLOBE. No one really
knows where to find him but those that have often
run into him when he is concealed in the deepness of a
dark night strolling around an empty ocean.

He is known as "Son of Abraham" and is accredit-
ed with having caused a lot of misery in people's lives.
When anyone meets him they are at a loss of words to
explain their history which has led them to search for
him. They are disappointed to learn that, it is indeed
true, he has nothing much to say but "You are here for
the love of your life." It matters not where you run into
him, that is all he says. It is of no consequence how
you phrase the question, that is all he offers. *You are
here for the love of your life.*

"Tell me something I don't know," once asked a
woman from New Mexico, initially in a composed whisper that was quickly followed by a trembling, *"Please."*

"I don't know what else to tell you."

She was in Kakakoy, in between Fethiye and Olu Deniz in southwestern Turkey, also known as "Ghost Village" to foreigners. She didn't know why she had desired to return to Fethiye and then Kakakoy for the third time.

"The love of my life doesn't want me. So how can I be here for the love of my life?"

Son of Abraham looked at her without seeing her face in the fog. He felt his old feet press and graze deeper into the mildly wet, soft sand. He decided to make an exception and elaborate.

"In the Navajo culture," he began, "there exists a Yeii Spirit." He continued, "A spirit considered by the Navajo to be a mediator between man and his creator. Yeiis control natural forces, such as day and night, rain, wind, sun and others. A very exceptional kind of yeii is the Yei'bi'chai, grandparent spirit or 'talking God' who can speak to man, teaching him how to live in harmony."

She tried to look for light in his eyes but it was too dark. She wanted more.

"Pay attention to my words: *the love of your life.*"

She would spend many miserable years looking for the love of her life in Turkey. But she was no exception. Anyone who met Son of Abraham spent despondent weeks, months, or years looking for the love of his or her life until they found the love–the love–in life.

Visceral Waves

Sleeplessly
I watch over
the spring night—
but no amount of guarding
is enough to make it stay.
—Izumi Shikibu

Sometimes he literally believed that he could exhale her into life. Right there. In front of him. And everything would carry on as they had always wanted.

Never understood why you always brought me by the water when you are afraid of it.

"I am not afraid when there is low tide. You can see things that you couldn't before. Besides, you are Mami Wata. Why would I fear the water with you around?"

No, you are the tide jewels, kanju and manju, *from Japanese mythology, the magical gems that the Sea God used to control the tides. You help control the tides to bring us here again and again.*

"No, tidal changes are the net result of multiple influences that act over varying periods. The combined effects of the gravitational forces exerted by the

Moon and the Sun and the rotation of the Earth. We can stand on something together when the moon does what it does, that's all; that's why I like to meet you here."

I like to see you in the sun.

"I like you with or without the sun."

I read something which made me think of your eyes.

"By?"

By Dorothea Grossman.

"What's it called?"

'I have to tell you.'

"When?"

No, that's what it's called!

"What?"

It's called 'I have to tell you.'

"Come closer before you do."

'I have to tell you, there are times when the sun strikes me like a gong, and I remember everything, even your ears.'

"Come closer."

Did you like it?

"Yes."

Except I remember your eyes, always.

"Don't be sad, please. We are here. We are together."

In your head.

"My head is real. My thoughts are real."

Why don't you just write your thoughts of me and send them to me instead?

"When I actually furnish my thoughts with words nothing comes out. That's when I stop thinking about you. I don't like to stop thinking about you."

We don't exist because of the net result of multiple influences that acted over a period.

Sometimes he literally believed that he could exhale her into life. Right there. In front of him. And everything would carry on as they had always wanted.

DAVINCI
dreams

Phantom Heart

"Of dreams: Men shall walk without moving, they shall hear those who are absent, they shall hear those that do not speak."
—from "Prophecies" by Leonardo Da Vinci, The Notebooks of Leonardo Da Vinci, George Braziller.

THE WATERS WHERE BOATS DOCK HARBOR A MURKY STILLNESS. Perhaps this is because light never quite reaches those corners where some boats never leave and others never return.

"She *fell* into the 'in between' world so I know who she is but I don't know who she is," Andreas whispered, his eyes stretching wide open as if held by thumbtacks. His eyebrows were deeply dark despite a head full of grays that resembled a thin silver sheet when combed back with Brylcream hair product.

"Everyone in town talks about you taking out two boats yet you won't let ma come with you."

"Because *she* is not your 'ma'. She is not *my* wife."

Although Litiya was familiar with this exchange with her father, she remained stumped by the hurt it caused her each time.

Eight years ago Litiya had accompanied her father

far out of their small harbor village to see a psychiatrist who specialized in "unusual neurological disorders" and who was in the capital city for a medical conference. Although doctors never saw patients during conferences, as was the custom in the profession, Litiya had requested a special arrangement with one of her friend's fathers who knew someone who knew the president of the university hosting the medical conference.

"Capgras' Delusion involves the distinct feeling that the people around you have been replaced by impostors," the American doctor had said. He had extended his stay for another week after the conference because he was genuinely intrigued by the symptoms and the disorder was a mere footnote in the profession.

"What do you mean 'delusion'?"

"Your father thinks your mother—his wife—is not his wife. She is replaced by another."

"I know that much. But how is this possible?"

"This can be brought about by a variety of conditions—changes in brain chemistry associated with different mental illnesses, or physical trauma to the brain—but really no one is certain of the underlying cause of Capgras."

"No one is certain of the cause of a disease…a disorder…?"

"Unfortunately, no."

"Then why even have it? That is absurd! On one end you are telling me my father is 'delusional', which means there is something wrong with him, and on another end you are saying no one knows why, and yet you even have a name for the symptom!" Litiya said, unable to place a lid on her bubbling anger and anxiety.

"Recent research has shown that it may be caused by psychological dissonance."

"What? What do you mean?"

"In some extreme cases, a change in the character of another or a newly noticed behavior can just be too difficult to accept, to integrate into the whole. And so, rather than reframing our sense of who that person is now, our brain just says, 'he or she must really be another.'"

"What? You really consider that a medical explanation?" Litiya tried to hold back her tears, recalling much of her mother's angst for the past eight years because her father had come home one day and said, "You look just like my Petka—but you are not my Petka. I know you are not."

"Well, there is the latest research which also says it could be a structural problem in the brain. When we see someone we know, a part of our brain called the fusiform gyrus identifies the face. That message is then sent to the amygdala, the part of the brain that activates the emotions we associate with that person. Patients who experience Capgras, in this one psychiatrist's view, the connection between visual recognition and emotional recognition is severed. So the patient is left with a convincing face but none of the accompanying feelings."

"How can we fix that?" Litiya asked, interested in the doctor's last explanation as closest to rational.

"We are so dependent on our emotional reactions

to the world around us that the visual perception is weak, and the brain's most logical compromise to rationalize is that another has been replaced by an "impostor". There has been one case where the patient was able to recognize the person speaking to them on the phone because our visual and auditory systems have different connections to the amygdala. But when the person appears face-to-face he is again labeled as an impostor."

"So there is no real solution," Litiya stated more than inquired, "This has been going on for eight years now."

"It's incredible really. Very rare." the doctor replied.

Litiya raised her eyes to meet the American doctor's and couldn't bring herself to wish him ill for his lack of interest in their ailments: how her mother cried herself to sleep every night for the first two years, how her father told the neighbors that his wife had been "snatched" from him and replaced by another who looked just like her, or how recently her father had started hearing his 'real' wife speak to him in his dreams despite the "impostor's presence in the other room."

"I am sorry. There is nothing more I can tell you. It is not like a phantom limb scenario. Every part of the body's surface has a corresponding point in the brain. So, let's say, once an arm is amputated the area in the brain mapped to the arm is deprived of sensory inputs it is used to receiving and so it becomes hungry for new sensations. This is not like that."

Hungry for new sensations...Litiya repeated the words without saying them aloud.

"We will be leaving now. Thank you very much for your time. My father and I appreciate your help," Litiya spoke without much thought.

Litiya and her father made the long journey back to their small village in Marmara Island. Outside of this "impostor" problem, Andreas was typical and loving. There was neither a significant change in his relationship with his daughter nor his friends with whom he fished and rented out boats as part of his small business.

Litiya admired her mother's perseverance to stay with Andreas no matter the challenges. Many women in the neighborhood had insisted she should separate. Litiya never once blamed her mother for not being able to pursue her university studies like her friends. Litiya had *wanted* to stay behind with her mother, or so she had said, often enough that she couldn't be convinced otherwise.

The American doctor didn't offer to share the anecdotes from his research that stated most who suffer from Capgras Delusion often emphatically insist that another "looks and acts just like the *real* person, but ... but... *some* essence of the person is missing, almost as though the 'soul' of the person isn't there." The doctor had refrained from sharing this information since he didn't quite believe in "soul."

When Litiya returned home, she didn't share everything that the American doctor had told her about Andreas. She kept it simple: "There is a structural problem in the brain and there is no fixing it."

After an early dinner Andreas went to "check on the boats" as he did every night. Petka hugged her daughter as she was doing the dishes, for understanding and caring. Litiya wanted to tell her mother that what hurt her the most was not what people said, or her inability to leave her parents to live her own life, or even Petka's loneliness, since she never knew what to expect when Andreas saw her each time—sometimes ignoring her and other times agitated and scared by her—but his recent sharing of dreams of the 'real' Petka. This 'real' Petka reminded Litiya of a mother that she barely recalled now, she was sure they weren't just dreams her father had had, lost memories anchored in a time when her mother truly felt alive.

Petka felt the painful silence in her daughter's eyes and the shoulders that wouldn't give into breath and finally said, "You know why I love boats? Most people can't tell one from another, yet if they love boats, they just love boats. I know your father loves me."

Neither Petka nor her mother addressed the fact that her father had been making boats since he was twelve and that eight years ago Petka too loved boats.

The Cradle of Stories

"Men shall speak with and touch and embrace each other while standing in different hemispheres, and shall understand each other's language."
—from "Prophecies" by Leonardo Da Vinci, The Notebooks of Leonardo Da Vinci, George Braziller.

ALL STORIES COME FROM FOG.

That is what Noor Baba told me.

A few years ago, on my way to explore Point Reyes National Seashore Park, I met a man named Noor Baba; I never made it to Point Reyes National Seashore Park that day, nor have I since.

Point Reyes National Seashore Park is a 70,000-acre national reserve which offers several beach walks and hiking. Point Reyes is a cape on the Pacific Coast of Northern California, approximately 30 miles northwest of San Francisco.

I used to live in San Francisco.

That is where I was headed, Point Reyes National Seashore Park, because it would do me "good", when I stopped for gas in the town of Point Reyes Station.

The town of Point Reyes Station, although not actually located on the peninsula, nevertheless provides most services to the vast Seashore Park, though some services are also available at nearby towns. The even smaller town of Olema, about 3 miles south of Point Reyes Station, serves as the standard starting point for a visit to the Point Reyes National Seashore Park.

Now I can't recall if I met Noor Baba in Olema or Point Reyes Station or between the two small towns.

Maybe I think I met him at Point Reyes Station only because I was at a fuel *station*.

Point Reyes Station is located along State Route 1. It is a small town that is recognized only because it holds a small population, barely 300 people; it lacks a separate municipal government or legal incorporation under the laws of the state of California.

"They filmed a movie there at Point Reyes National Seashore Park back in the 1980's—some stupid story because fog is supposed to scare you," that is what Noor Baba said after I told him where I was headed.

Although the fog had not impeded visibility yet, it was descending quicker than I had anticipated. Having lived in the San Francisco Bay area I was used to fog but I had been warned that it gets 'pretty bad' around Point Reyes.

"I haven't seen that movie," I had replied.

Noor Baba's skin was paler than mine and I know I am a very white guy. Close African-American friends even jokingly call me 'whitey,' that is how white I am. But his paleness, unlike mine, was a patchwork of rosy cheeks and mountain wrinkles spread proportionately throughout his round face. He could suit up for Santa

Clause and I would remain invisible, one of many. I don't usually notice men's eyes but I just couldn't help staring at his. The soft pale blue shade was frosty and burst forth as if the horizon was staring across at you instead of you looking up at the sky.

I waited for the gas tank to fill up as Noor Baba decided to clean my car's windshield. I noticed his dirty uniform and the oil underneath his nails. I didn't ask him how long he had been working at this fuel station.

I felt bad that a man twice my age was cleaning the windshield on a car that was old enough to retire in a junk yard but I didn't say anything, recalling my father's voice when I would have to clean his car as a young boy, "Everyone has a job to do."

The bulls of memory are strong. I don't know why I thought of my father that day given that he had passed away over ten years ago.

"So, you from here?" I asked him given the silence was as wet as the foggy air.

"Yes, some three towns down. Not a bad commute if there is no fog. But usually the hour I have to come in there is always fog."

I detected a slight accent but didn't inquire.

"It's a lovely place to go explore if it doesn't get too foggy. Some times it can get very foggy," Noor Baba said. I appreciated his attempt at conversation. I wondered how desperate I looked.

"Yes, that is what I am doing. Came here because some colleagues said it would do me good. After they shared the news with me that I was just let go from my job."

"Let go?"

"Yes, as in fired, but not really. It's a long story."

Noor Baba nodded but I don't think he understood anything other than that I was fired.

Some lies are spontaneous; others are planned. I think the spontaneous lies are most adjacent to the truth. The truth was I had quit my job two years ago, the same year my ex-girlfriend left me because *she* couldn't "handle" that I still wanted to be with her in spite of her being diagnosed with terminal cancer. She died a year later, now a year ago.

Job or no job didn't matter. I made ends meet going as far as my car could go around this great land that is apparently not enough for our government.

"So what are you going to do now?" Noor Baba asked.

"I don't know."

"Well, you have family to support?"

"No. No. Nothing of the sort. Luckily."

"How is that lucky?"

"Well, I mean, I don't have to worry about others you know?"

"It is lucky to worry about others," Noor Baba replied.

I changed the subject. "Where are you from? You don't sound like you are from here?"

"Oh. Originally originally? From Afghanistan," he said and smiled at my surprise.

"The country with the war going on?"

"There are many countries with a war going on. I

am from one such country, yes."

Noor Baba had been in northern California for the last seventeen years and had not returned to see his wife and children for the last eight, given there was a "war going on."

"But I talk to my wife every day. Every day," he said proudly. "After Obama gets elected I should be able to visit her again."

I didn't know what to say. I didn't even believe Barak Obama would get elected.

"Well, that is good that you still talk to her. My girlfriend of four years left me given I couldn't see her for two weeks."

"Girlfriend? Four years and she wasn't your wife?"

"Well, I mean that stuff takes some time you know," I replied and decided he didn't understand due to cultural differences. I was overcome by the fact that I was lying to this stranger, all the way from Afghanistan standing in front of me in the middle of a town recognized only for census, while there was a war going on.

"Well, women don't come back. You want her you have to go back. Or maybe you will find a new one," Noor Baba said jovially.

"I wanted to write a story or something like that about her now that I don't have a job," I said truthfully.

I quickly tried to dismiss the recollection that flashed unexpectedly, as it often did, of the day I learned Alina had died.

I fell to my knees after my mother had called to

tell me the news and I couldn't force any tears and felt angry for not being able to cry. It was then I realized praying would never be enough. And just like people have a moment where they can distinctly recall feeling "Grace" or "something" that changes them into a believer of "God," that was my moment to stop believing.

I saw the sky in Noor Baba's eyes stare at the volcano inside me.

"All stories come from the fog. You can't do much though, if you are afraid of what you can't see," he finally said.

My gas tank had been full for quite a few minutes.

I reached for my wallet without intending to go inside the station to pay.

"While fog is a type of a cloud, the term 'fog' is typically distinguished from the more generic term 'cloud' in that fog is low-lying, and the moisture in the fog is often generated locally such as from a nearby body of water, like a lake or the ocean, or from nearby moist ground," Noor Baba said.

He continued, "Shadows are cast through fog in three dimensions. The fog is dense enough to be illuminated by light that passes through gaps in a structure or tree, but thin enough to let a large quantity of that light pass through to illuminate points further on."

He paused to say hello to someone who passed by that I didn't even notice and then he proceeded, "Fog can form in a number of ways and there are many types of fogs. Fog is a reflection of our hydrosphere, found on, under, and over the surface of this planet in many different forms before it actually becomes what we call fog. Stories, like fog, are a continuum encircling this Earth."

He told me it was probably not a good idea to drive to the Point Reyes National Seashore Park now.

"You should stay at some place around here because it will be too foggy to come back safely," he said.

"Yes, I think so. Don't want a foggy story," I tried to joke.

He didn't laugh.

"Men don't lie about things they know little about," Noor Baba said.

I wondered why I was unable to tell any truth to a stranger I was never going to see again.

"Stories are the saints of desperate cases and lost causes," said Noor Baba.

I still don't know whether I believe in saints, angels, or a God, but I believe in stories because I am a desperate case. And maybe not a lost cause just yet.

Time Blur

"Of the lights carried before the dead: they will make light for the dead."
—from "Prophecies" by Leonardo Da Vinci, The Notebooks of Leonardo Da Vinci, George Braziller.

I ONCE ASKED SARBAND "HOW DO LEAVES DRY?" and she, being hard of hearing at her age, heard "How do leaves die?"

"They don't die!" she replied, more agitated than I would have expected regardless of the question. She continued, "The plant or the tree kills them off! Become a burden. Not as efficient as they age."

Sarband always held onto the broom as if the broomstick really could do more than sweep the dock.

"Some leaves just change colors and wake up again though. Some are recycled to go back as food for the roots. Those leaves the light can no longer reach or they can't make much of the light that comes to them must shed though, regardless what becomes of them," Sarband added.

Ever since I can recall while living next to Sarband she has been old; so I don't know exactly how old she is. When I was twelve I used to wish she would not be out cleaning the area around the deck because if she saw me she would not stop talking. That is also when I decided if I was going to get old—at twelve you think you have a choice—I was not going to talk a lot. I even have a journal entry from other seemingly hollow accounts of those days, "I am never going to be one of those old people who never shuts up when they are old."

September 15:
I want to be like my grandma old. She never says a word.

When Sarband asked "How are you doing?" it always meant Sarband had to tell you how you and others *should* be doing, sometimes that included *what* we should be doing. "You all young kids—shit, not just you kids but your parents—need to upkeep this area. It can't just be us old folks who do this, you know."

September 18:
Why do old people talk so much? I am twelve. It is okay if I talk a lot. I have different things to say. I try to pay attention so I don't say the same thing again and again. Old people keep repeating the same things.

When I returned after my first year of college Sarband told me how she was organizing with the various local community boards to do something about the neighborhood. "They are just tearing up these trees to make room for development. They call it development. But we know what is really developing: their money!" Her extremely light skin belied her ethnicity but she never asserted that to begin with. Not that I can recall. She proclaimed many other causes quite explicitly though, all having to do with the neighborhood or the district. Only sometimes were racial issues weaved into these aims.

September 23rd:
Mother says she wishes grandma would talk more. I don't know why. Does she know what it would be like if we had a Sarband in the house? Jessica in my class says both her grandmothers live with her. I only have one, thank God! And double thanks that she is not like Sarband, always with something to say!

After college Sarband wanted to know when I was getting married. I had moved back home because I couldn't find a job with my unofficial Viticulture and Enology degree. Now Cornell offers it as a proper degree, which few pursue, but I just made up a major back then so it was to be expected I would not have a job despite having graduated from Cornell. Viticulturists are often intimately involved with winemakers because vineyard management and the resulting grape characteristics provide the basis from which winemaking can begin. No one in our house drank, not even wine. I told Sarband when I had a job that's when I would get married.

Sarband said, "Find a good woman first, it will make you find a good job."

"Things are different now. No woman will even date you if you don't have a job."

"Things ain't that different," Sarband replied. "If she loves you, she will," Sarband said and added cynically, "and if she *really* loves you she'll make sure you get one. Trust that." she continued,

"Now it's gonna be tough luck finding a job with that grape degree of yours."

"Yes, I know. I don't know what I was thinking."

"You probably weren't. But you will figure it out. I see that about you."

Sarband was right. I hadn't been thinking. I had met an Indian girl at Cornell that I was dating my third year. She took me to a meditation in a temple once where we sat down and the woman leading the meditation—not Indian but some Caucasian not from New York—handed us these raisins. We sat there holding these raisins with our eyes closed. She asked us to feel the texture of the raisin. We did that for a few minutes. Then she told us to imagine the raisin is our skin. I began pressing harder than I had been. After a few minutes that woman asked us to feel the texture of the raisin as if it was our insides. I realized I had obliterated the raisin, compressing it between my index finger and thumb with such force that it was flattened without any form.

The meditation teacher told us to open our eyes and said, "The way you moved your fingers to feel the texture of the raisin is your relationship with your memories."

After that I just wanted to study grapes instead

of myself.

Sarband continued, "Let me tell you about my husband and his first experience at a real vineyard... you know what a real vineyard is, right?"

I knew. I had heard this story last year too.

September 28th:
I wonder if Sarband talks a lot because no one listens to her. That is not true, though. I have seen her talk a lot to other people. And she has grandkids. They are much older than me though. Like, they are my parents old.

"So now you are upstate?" Sarband asked although she knew I had moved a few years ago. "The politics upstate are way different than in the city. I bet you miss the City."

I did but it was a job.

Sarband continued her cleaning of the deck when she talked. Sometimes she even brushed the neighbors' decks, including ours. She said if the whole row of houses wasn't tidy who was going to look at her grandson's place even if his deck and front yard were sparkling.

October 5th:
Grandma is sick. I keep hearing mother and her boyfriend say she is too young to die. I thought she was old.

Once I returned home without having visited in five years. I would just have my mother and step-sister fly to where I was in the world. Interestingly, we always brought up Sarband, even if only briefly.

"I watched this show the other day. These people go SCAD diving. SCAD stands for "suspended catch air device." It is like bungee jumping without the bungee. You dangle by a cable about 150 feet off the ground, facing up to the sky, then click and you are released and you land in a net about 3 seconds later. Did you know about this?"

I didn't.

"So I did some research and learned that this neuroscientist, I forget his name, I am getting old, but I will remember it, does research on how our brains perceive and understand time. He did an experiment where he used SCAD diving. He has written some articles on why a sudden brush with death or dying-like experiences make things go in slow-motion. He says our 'memories are like sieves.' We accumulate a tremendous amount of memory in an unusually short amount of time without even knowing it. Most stimuli never become part of our memory like the ones we can recall easily. Like, a memory easily recalled would be when you majored in grapes. But when we have a near death experience, or anything that which shifts the brain's gears, the brain starts to write everything down, every cloud, piece of dirt, smile from a stranger. The scientist thinks the slow-motion effect is our brain's way of making sense of all this extra information that we didn't even know was stored."

I had to go; as expected I was going to be late because I had run into Sarband. Sarband. Always cleaning the leaves on the deck.

November 15th:
Grandma died. She wasn't even that old.

Sarband is quite old now but I feel more tired than her. She still talks a lot. She is happy to know I finally married and actually have three children of my own. We sold our house that was next to Sarband's grandson. My mother is no longer with us. I never really have a reason to stop by our neighborhood.

"Old people who talk a lot end up living a lot longer," Sarband said to me the last time I stopped by the neighborhood and she told me why leaves die. Then she quietly added, "We have to."

"There are many ways to die, Lucas, and there are many near death-experiences that go unnoticed."

I am learning to talk. A lot.

Quietus

*"Of the shadow that moves with: there shall be seen
shapes and figures of men and animals which shall pursue these men and animals wheresoever they flee; and the
movements of the one shall be as those of the other, but it
shall seem a thing to wonder at because of the different
dimensions which they assume."*
—from "Prophecies" by Leonardo Da Vinci, The
Notebooks of Leonardo Da Vinci, George Braziller

"Is he a God?"

"A *God*? Have you lost your damn mind entirely?"
Frank answered and then immediately regretted his
choice of words.

"I probably have," replied Merrick.

"Come on, man. I didn't mean it like that. I just
meant—"

"No, you are right. Only someone who has lost
his bearings would even ask that, even as a joke, given
the circumstances," said Merrick.

Frank couldn't help thinking maybe insanity and
death weren't so far apart after all: both made one
reach out to some unknown entity, God by whatever
name, regardless if one had ever prayed or believed be-

forehand. This thought was followed by the quick re-alization that he had inferred that Merrick's problems, his friend of thirty years, fell on some spectrum of a mental illness. Frank then realized he had referred to Merrick's experiences as problems and just wished he could stop thinking.

Frank recalled what his ex-wife had once said: it is the devil that leads one to God, and he and Merrick both "attract evil, evil, evil, so I pray it is only so as to lead you both one day to meet God while still alive." The divorce was finalized twenty years ago and Frank was disappointed to find himself thinking of that par-ticular exchange, especially now.

Frank couldn't help thinking maybe his ex-wife was right, that Merrick's callous womanizing (not all resulted in physical affairs) over the last fifteen years had finally led to this identity crisis where his dreams haunted him. He felt as if he was not even alive, that he was dead and just an observer, that maybe his ex-wife, who Frank had never considered religious before he married her, was right that what you do to others "starts eating your insides."

Merrick wasn't a bad man and in fact had done many kind things for many people, Frank considered; it was just that ever since he could recall, Merrick had had a way with women—some due to his appearance, which was handsome by most standards, but that was irrelevant since time never offered favors to anyone—and he didn't hesitate to assert this side of him, the side to which Frank could never relate. The side that always divided them as Frank-but-Merrick ever since he had known him. Merrick had married once and the duration of the marriage—six months—ensured he never took that risk again. "It's not for me," Merrick had said.

The two friends didn't see each other as often when Frank was married for ten years. "It's different when you care about someone, Merrick," Frank used to say.

Apparently, didn't care enough, Frank thought and again wished he could freeze his thoughts.

The two men cut through the frozen wind trying to reach Vishuddha Creek. The track was frozen over with ice on top of old snow and although both men were dressed in proper attire to combat the gusts of wind, the cold was still abrasive against the uncovered parts of their face.

"He is not a *god*. Some retired neurobiologist," Frank said without adding "also considered quite deranged according to many valid sources."

Merrick ignored that information and asked, "Why did we have to leave at four in the morning in this forsaken cold?"

"Because G. R. S. can only be found or decides to come out and about near the Creek when it turns blue," Frank said and then continued, "So by the time it would take us to get there it would almost be evening and around that time."

"Why do you call him G.R.S.?" snapped Merrick.

"That's his name. That's what he goes by."

"Those are his *initials*."

"I don't know anyone who refers to him otherwise. I don't even know what the 'R' stands for."

"Let's call him Gary. Or Garreth. Rings like Merrick," Merrick said.

"That doesn't sound like Merrick and he has two first names anyway. How am I going to call him Gary if there is another name he prefers?"

Merrick almost said aloud, "Great. Going to a nut case like myself," but didn't, given his last exchange with Frank before they had boarded the plane. Frank had said, "I went through a lot to find out where this man is, Merrick, and the only thing I was told was you have to believe—whatever he does or has to say—it doesn't work."

Merrick had argued, "But I don't believe in God, Frank! What do you want me to believe?! That some neurobiologist who once worked with the likes of Roger Wolcott Sperry's team and eventually went crazy is somehow to fix this–this–all of this?!"

At that instant Frank threw the boarding pass down on the floor and said, "You don't have to believe in God or something like God in order to believe, Merrick! Just believe you want to be fixed."

The two men paused to eat. As they had been advised there was nothing—no person selling anything, no cabin, no restaurant, no houses—between the small village where they were staying and Vishuddha Creek so it was best to pack their own food supply.

Merrick couldn't believe how exhausted he was and that made him angry: even walking against wind was a fight.

"I wonder if these trees are even half alive in this

frozen weather?" Merrick said after taking a bite of his sandwich, immediately disliking the taste. His options had been lamb curry wrapped in flat bread or potato curry wrapped in spicy flat bread. He had said "whichever" to the young girl—the guesthouse keeper's daughter—knowing both were going to taste awful when eaten cold in the cold.

"Of course they are; they wouldn't be standing otherwise," said Frank as he took out the canteen provided by the guesthouse owner for a drink of water.

"You think we are paying too much for that guesthouse? It's not even really a guesthouse, or lodge, or inn, you know. Just someone's house."

"What does it matter? Lucky someone took us in around these parts where they don't even speak to strangers, especially in our skin."

"Just saying. They knew we needed a place to stay and there was no where else to stay, like those touristy towns nearby, given where we were headed in the morning."

Frank and Merrick finished the rest of their lunch in silence and heard the snapping and fizzing of branches crackling in spite of the ice and snow over them. Frank couldn't help thinking that trees made sounds even when frozen so as to affirm being alive.

They continued to walk, which required even more attention, since their hiking boots were a weak match for the slippery iced path and the sun was hidden behind the trees.

"You don't have Cotard's syndrome—the delusion where one has no sense of being alive in the moment, the disorder where you think you are dead although you are very much alive." That was Merrick's first diagnosis. That was a year ago.

"You don't have temporal lobe epilepsy which can give sufferers an experience called transient epileptic amnesia, which is a fancy way of saying the world around them stays just as real and vivid – in fact, even more vivid sometimes – but they have no sense of who they are. You have a very fine sense of who you are, Merrick." That was Merrick's second attempt at understanding his mental state.

"You don't have any neural pathology to experience the separation of sense of self and conscious experience, Merrick. I have been in this field for a long time. Lots of people who use—" Merrick didn't even allow that particular doctor to finish the evaluation and had stormed out screaming: "I don't use any drugs" followed by a string of expletives.

It was six months later when Frank gave Merrick an article about an experiment with "split-brain" patients of a neurobiologist named Roger Sperry.

As a last resort in an experimental procedure to treat severe epilepsy, Sperry's team severed the connection (the corpus callosum) between the two hemispheres of the brain. The results of this operation, called a commissurotomy, was that the epilepsy was indeed much reduced but the experiments also revealed a remarkable, unforeseen side effect.

Patients were asked to focus on a dot in the centre of a screen. Words and images were then flashed up for a few seconds on either the right or left side of the screen. When these appeared on the right side of the screen, the patients were easily able to say what they were. But when they appeared on the left of the screen, they claimed to have seen nothing. However, if asked to draw an object with their left hand, they would draw what they had just seen, all the time denying they had seen any such thing. They could also manipulate or use the object normally with their left hands.

The way in which vision works is that information from the right visual field is processed by the left brain hemisphere, while information from the left visual field is processed by the right hemisphere. But it is the left hemisphere that (in most people) controls speech. Because normally the corpus callosum allows the two hemispheres to communicate, this presents no practical difficulty for most people. But after a commissurotomy, this information exchange cannot occur. That means that if you control carefully which side of the brain receives information from the environment, you can effectively make one hemisphere aware of something that the other is not. What is astonishing about this is that for this to be possible, there would have to be two centers of awareness in the individual concerned. Commissurotomy therefore seems to show that selves can be divided – at least temporarily – or that they needn't have just one centre of consciousness after all.

Intriguingly, however, in normal life, such patients experience the world in the normal, unified way. One of Roger Sperry's closest students and team members offered the following explanation: "we don't miss what we no longer have access to." Consciousness of self emerges from a network of thousands or millions of conscious moments. This means that when we lose bits, the way a split-brain patient does, we don't sense anything as lost at all.

In other words, what the numerous pathologies of self-experience expose is that even in normal cases, there is no unified "I" behind experience. Rather, to use another musical metaphor, the mind is like a jazz orchestra that usually plays with sufficient harmony to disguise the fact that it lacks a single player, a score, or even a conductor. A few bum notes or absent musicians, however, and the illusion is shattered.

Merrick felt the article, which had been opened, read and folded many times over, in the inside pocket of his jacket. It had taken him and Frank six months to plan this trip to see a less renowned member of the Sperry team who had worked on the split-brain experiment. No one still living and working in the field at any of the universities was interested in entertaining Merrick's insomnia, sense of loss of self, and dreams that led into visions through the waking hours.

Frank looked at Merrick quickly.

"What are you looking at?"

"Nothing. We are almost there. Just have to find the bluest area in order find him."

"There is no telling if he will be there. We may have to go back and do this all over again."

"I know this," Merrick replied.

The aquamarine reflection of the water in the creek was a breathtaking sight that neither was expecting.

"Wow. This is some creek. There is a current despite how frozen it is," Frank said.

"Now. Where do we find this G.R.S.?"

"No idea."

"We wait?"

Frank and Merrick both turned around upon hearing, "It would be quite cruel to make two men wait in this cold after that long hike, no?"

There he was. G.R.S. As ordinary looking as any man.

"You were expecting us?" Frank asked.

"No. But when you see people around the creek this time of the year they are usually lost or foreigners, and I know that hike," G.R.S. replied.

"We—I—need to see you about something," Merrick said quickly.

"There is a town up that way which offers housing for the night—" G.R.S. began.

"We are not tourists. I came to see you," Merrick said, cutting G.R.S. short.

"Me? Most people don't even know who I am or where I am."

"It took a lot—six months—research to guess where you might be."

The old man sat down to fill water in a large container from the running current as the sun highlighted the frozen parts, along with the flowing current, an electric, indigo shade of blue. Frank gestured Merrick to go over to him and Merrick went closer to G.R.S. but remained standing.

Frank listened to the conversation, the details of

Merrick's experiences now familiar as though his own.

"There is nothing wrong with you. Someone just gave you a virus. Dreams can be like a virus. Like a cold."

"What?"

"Dreams like the one you describe are like viruses. You just catch them. Like a cold. Some colds continue to stay inside you to mutate into another cold. No two colds are alike, though."

"But how does one get this virus?"

"Being in a familiar place even if you don't recall having been there in any memory. A rainy night that reminds you of another place. A small glimpse that triggers a familiar memory. No telling, really. How do you catch a cold? It just happens. Nothing to do with your hair being too wet. Someone just gives it to you. And the virus finds another body."

Merrick couldn't believe this.

"It's a way of shedding one's shadow."

"Whose shadow? These dreams are someone's shadow?

"Some of them. It is like passing on a baton made of burdens."

"Don't I have to know someone or something to be experiencing these?" Merrick said, quite worried. None of this made any sense to him, yet it was the only explanation that had made any sense in years.

"Well, yes, but there is no way to find out who or what," G.R.S. replied. "Some dreams, like some stories, suck us deeper than we can stand," he added and then chuckled.

"What's so amusing?"

"That you actually thought after reading that article and reading about me that I could help you or fix you," G.R.S. replied.

At this point Frank interrupted the conversation, "I know of a man who said he found you and you helped him."

"He lied," G.R.S. retorted.

"How do I get rid of this?" Merrick asked, agitated.

"It will pass."

"No. It won't. It hasn't. This has been going on for a year."

"Then you figure it out by living them out."

"This sense of self and duality I feel has left me feeling insane. The only friend I have left is Frank. No one understands. No one! I don't even know if I exist! I have no idea what is real anymore. I have led a meaningful life, worked hard, cared for others. Sure, I may not be the best in relationships, but I have been better than I used to be! The more my dreams become real the less I understand what is happening! You helped someone else! You help me!" Merrick finally stopped.

It was completely dark now. G.R.S. lit a lantern and appeared much more infirm now than he had before.

G.R.S. finally said, "You know that a cube is a three-dimensional object that casts a shadow which appears as two-dimensional. Poor cube, a three-dimensional object that has not been represented in its projection properly! But that is the cost of losing a dimension. Just like that, although we can't see a four-dimensional object we can see its shadow as a three-dimensional object and therefore know it exists. Dreams are like that."

"What the hell do these dreams want?"

"Death. Death of something that causes killing."

It would be a few years before Merrick would understand there were many different kinds of killings but by then he had, without knowing, offered the baton made of dreams to another.

THAIS stories

Four Sides

"One part of the authentic self wanders light years out in the interstellar spaces, in exile from us. The other part is buried so deep within us that to resurrect it would be another return from exile.
—Harold Bloom

MORE THAN 3,500 YEARS AGO, 100 MILES WEST OF LUXOR AND 300 MILES SOUTH OF CAIRO, there was a road next to the ancient Girga Road known as Bin Abas. It was one of the many roads which led to nowhere. Sometimes it brought the pedestrians back to where they began and other times some of these small pathways led elsewhere. No traveler was quite the same when they did finally make their way around.

Thais was one such passerby.

A tableaux of scenes and symbols can be found on the walls surrounding Bin Abas illustrating four sides of her story.

One story holds that she came looking for Goddess Maat, the Ancient Egyptian principle of truth, order and justice.

Another story states that she was in love with

Sinuhe, who holds life of Sycamore trees.

The third story reveals that her name wasn't even Thais and was in fact a young man who often got lost.

The fourth story is the most complex. The carvings reveal a disturbing tale which many from the area still regard as a possibility.

Thais met a seventeen year-old boy one afternoon who asked her directions to Girga Road because he didn't know how to get there on his own. Thais, older and more experienced than him, told the boy a shorter route was possible through Bin Abas. The boy had short brown hair, darker brown eyes, and wore a long white linen shirt with a blue scarf wrapped around the middle. The light colors made his skin appear darker than it really was.

They say it was the bone-dehydrating heat of the desert and the boy never made it to Girga Road.

It was shortly after that Thais began speaking in fours. She had four names and four stories for all her selves.

It would have scared the townspeople, but she was usually accurate in her four perspectives of herself.

Thais lived like this for a long time. No one knew her age.

That was a long time ago.

Eventually someone who was scared of her many selves brutally murdered Thais.

Now the world has many unauthentic four sides striving to be one, which is not possible.

Gravity

YOUR SHADOW IS THE REASON YOU CANNOT FLY. IT'S HEAVIER THAN YOU KNOW.

Thais, like most children of her time, could fly ever since she was little.

Some researchers and a few distrusted scientists believe there is evidence to suggest that humans achieved flight earlier in history—much earlier—so early, they say, that the knowledge of this technology has been lost and ancient stories that recount adventures of human flight have been relegated only to myth.

In 1898, a peculiar six-inch wooden object was found in a tomb in Saqquara, Egypt which dated back to 200 BCE. The object had a body or fuselage, seven-inch wings that curved downward slightly, a fixed rudder and a tail. It looked very much like a modern airplane or glider. But since airplanes had not yet been invented in 1898 it was labeled as a model of a bird and stored away in the basement of the Cairo museum.

The object was rediscovered many years later by Dr. Khalil Messiha, an authority on ancient models. According to Messiha and others who studied the object, it had characteristics of a very advanced aerodynamics, much like modern pusher-gliders that require very little power to stay aloft. The curved wings are today known as reverse dihedral wings which can attain great amounts of lift. A similar design is employed on the supersonic Concorde aircraft.

The researchers argue that this discovery could possibly have been a child's toy or a scale model of an aircraft the Egyptians planned to build. Some say they did in fact build it although no conclusive evidence exists to show for it.

Egypt isn't the only ancient civilization that has produced puzzling artifacts. A remarkable gold trinket estimated to be at least 1,000 years old – dating perhaps to between 500 and 800 AD – was found in Central America and along coastal areas of South America. If you weren't aware of its age, you might guess that it was a child's model of the Space Shuttle or a delta wing fighter aircraft. When the artifact was discovered, archaeologists called it a zoomorph, or animal-shaped object. It resembles no known flying animal, however.

Then there are huge works of art drawn on the ground by people of the Paracas and Nasca cultures. These can be found over a 37 by 15 mile plateau near Nazca, Peru. The figures, called geoglyphs, are stylized portraits of 18 different kinds of birds, a curly-tailed monkey as big as a football field, a killer whale, a 150-foot spider, a lizard, human forms and other strange objects. They can only be viewed in their entirety from the sky.

*

Thais was not half-bird; she was born out of the wind. She wasn't really born out of the wind; it is just a fancy way of saying no one really knew where her people came from. People near the ancient Girga Road in Egypt often create ornamental ways of stating facts they don't understand but consider worthy of noting.

So, it was only natural that she could fly. The space of confluence where the ocean honors the shore before dissolving and returning is where children like Thais want to experience their first flight. The shadow is not as heavy near the ocean because the waves carry parts of us we don't comprehend.

There were others who could fly too; Thais just knew how to work with gravity better. Thais was more apt at flying because she understood that in order to work with gravity you have to understand the Earth.

Eventually, some tribal leaders demanded that Thais's elders honestly explain how she could defy gravity or else they would consider her possessed by the Jinn people, and have her arms amputated.

Jinn people are those who are before history, not quite visible or known to civilization, strangers you can't recognize easily. In some religious texts they are referenced as having seen it all before.

Thais did her best as a young child to explain that one could only fly if free and that there was nothing supernatural to it. She explained it as the "soul of the world" flowing through you, where the laws were defined by One.

This only disturbed the tribal leaders even more, and they demanded more honesty. Since no amount of truth was enough, Thais's elders were informed that the following morning her arms would be cut off so as to prevent the sorcery.

They say that Thais cried so much that night that the following morning she couldn't open her eyes. It took a month to open them and see again.

The next morning Thais spoke honestly to keep her arms intact. After that she only spoke honestly about her pain, that night, the interrogations, and what she remembered of flying.

And that is how the myth of freedom was created: honesty at the expense of truth.

No human could fly thereafter because honesty casts a heavy shadow that the ocean can't suspend against gravity, for honesty doesn't go beyond the personal.

Maat

BEFORE THERE WERE MOTHERS THERE WERE TREES.

The aforementioned fact is well known to all people who know such truth-learnings.

Ancient plants made it out of water 130 million years *prior* to the discovery of earth's first modern tree, which was 370 million years ago. Archaeopteris is an extinct tree that made up 90% of the forests. It took over a 100 million years for certain evolutionary features in Archaeopteris to attain trunks up to 3 feet wide and stand 60 to 90 feet tall. The features included rings—to support greater and greater height and weight—bringing nutrients all the way from the insides of the earth to the farthest leaves, supportive collars of extra wood, and internal layers which dovetail at branches to prevent breakage.

Maat was a direct descendant of those who drank the sap of the most ancient tree.

Originally, she was just someone who was in harmony with the trees, stars, seasons, and the actions of both mortals and those considered deities. Her purpose was nothing more than to bring order to the universe from chaos at the moment of creation. Her male counter-part they say was Thoth, a deity often considered as the heart, which, according to the ancient Egyptians near Girga Road, is the seat of intelligence or the mind. Together they stood for Truth and Maat specifically oversaw balance, morality, and justice borne out of that Truth.

Because she was a descendant of the most ancient tree, she understood that she and Thoth were just guardians of Truth and not necessarily arbitrators of it. However, many people, both the ancient rulers and the governed alike, decided to worship Maat. The Kings referred to her as a Goddess and others incorporated variations of her name into their own names or created rituals to have her influence in their lives.

She tried to explain that a nation is enlightened only if The Power of the State accepts being subservient to the core values of truth, balance, equality and justice, and that the source of these values is not her but the Oneness found in trees.

No one really knows how Maat died or if she had any children. Her influence lasted long after her, but eventually she and her words were forgotten given that it is human nature to forget, even to its own detriment.

So it was a surprise to the entire village surrounding Girga Road in ancient Egypt, when a girl named Thais, only twelve years old, had a dream about a tree and a woman named Maat. If this dream was like others that children of that time period had, it could be ignored, but there was a change in Thais after the recurring dreams about Maat. She was withdrawn from most children, often stared at adults as if they were ghosts, and spent most of her time talking to trees.

Her mother sought the advice of the elders in the village and they recommended several treatments. One such treatment included dunking the child's head underwater near the village river to clear out dreams. Her mother understood the risk associated: a child could die. The elders said it was better to be saved by death than live a life of haunted dreams.

Thais's mother consulted her husband and her own mother and the mother's sisters. One of the elder-mothers told of a story of this Bedouin woman who traveled to their parts from far away. She had heard that this Bedouin woman had answers to dreams. The problem was that no one knew when she visited. Thais's mother decided to wait.

The world is not easily understanding of those who wait. The villagers believed Thais was a threat given her prior history several years ago, which had included a long trial—the youngest child ever placed on trial—to honestly explain how she thought she could fly.

Despite being ostracized, Thais's mother held strong and waited for the day she would meet the Bedouin gypsy.

The day came when whispers were exchanged near the fire-lit lanterns of several tents that a Bedouin from the Rub Al-Khali desert had finally arrived. She had many goats but only one was white and it only had half a horn above the left eye. Whispers have legs and find their way to the right ears if they are listening.

The very next day Thais's mother arranged to

meet the Bedouin gypsy from the Rub Al-Khali desert. There was a long line as there were many people who wanted to understand their dreams. Finally, Thais's turn came.

"I want you to tell her about Maat—tell her everything Thais. She can help you," Thais's mother said gently to her daughter.

The gypsy, like most Bedouin Arab women of the Desert was covered, only her dark kholed eyes showed through the two holes that were open on the cloth that covered her face and the rest of her body. The gypsy came out of her tent. Thais gasped.

They stared at each other.

Finally, Thais spoke first, "I am here to tell you about dreams of a woman named Maat."

"Your mother will die soon, Thais," instead replied the Bedouin gypsy.

Thais stood still. She couldn't comprehend "soon" but she knew her mother was still alive and waiting for her outside the tent, so she was relieved to conclude that "soon" could not mean now.

"I need you to understand that Maat knew she knew the Truth and wasn't afraid of what she knew. The spirit of Maat finds her way to those who can echo Truth."

"I don't know any truth. I can't even fly anymore."

"You will have to re-learn everything you will try to forget."

"What's going to happen to my mother? My mother's mother is old. Why can't my mother be that old with me?"

"No one knows when mothers become trees, but they do."

"I am here to understand why I dream of Maat," Thais said, not liking what she heard.

"You also dream of trees," replied the Bedouin gypsy woman, and added, "All those who carry any part of the Truth are mothers. You will find your mother again, even if she or he doesn't look like how you remember her now."

Trees bring all of the harmony from the bottom of the ocean to the earth and beyond. We have paper made from trees on which we paint, draw, doodle, write, another can understand a part of Truth that Maat knew too well: we are all guardians.

It wasn't long thereafter that Thais's mother passed away. But unlike Maat, Thais was not ready to unfurl along with any truth.

Thais, like most people, would spend years forgetting only to later search to remember.

The Bridge

Capital "T" Truth
*A new scientific truth does not triumph by convincing
its opponents and making them see the light, but rather
because its opponents eventually die, and a new generation grows up that is familiar with it.*
—Max Plank

BEFORE THAIS WAS INTERESTED IN ARCHITECTURE
SHE HAD AN AMBITIOUS INTEREST IN PHYSICS.

Thais became engrossed in physics after reading a
paper published in 1933 by the Swiss astronomer Fritz
Zwicky showing that visible matter is only a small fraction of the universe. She learned that just 18 percent
of the matter in the universe is composed of the mate-
rial we know and that the remaining 82 percent con-
stitutes 'dark matter'.

Dark matter is made of a type of particle that
doesn't like to interact with normal matter very often
and it is very heavy and very massive. It is rather difficult to find dark matter given it doesn't interact much
with other particles, to search for it is to wait for a
particle of dark matter to come into contact with other
matters in detector machines.

Thereafter, Thais left her studies in Cairo to learn more about dark matter.

She came across many astronomers in Geneva, Switzerland who reinforced this view. Thais learned that the presence of dark matter helps explain why our galaxy is stable. Having been brought up near the ancient Girga Road in Egypt, she already knew The Milky Way is a disk that rotates like a merry-go-around and what keeps it from flying apart is gravity. There isn't enough *visible* matter in the galaxy to account for the amount of gravity needed to hold it together, hence the existence of 'dark matter.'

"That is how we know that there must be other matter there that we can't see."

Sometimes a sentence, like saying a particular name, is a falsetto that continues to reverberate through our core.

Thais couldn't focus on her physics studies thereafter and chose not to finish her research in astronomy. Instead, she left for Abruzzo, Italy, the region's western border resting less than 50 miles east of Rome.

Her neighbor, a student of philosophy, had once casually mentioned a man named Gus somewhere in Abruzzo who knew of a different dark matter. It was said that Gus was an old man who was a direct descendant of the Praetutii, who were an ancient tribe of central Italy. Thais didn't expect to find Gus but she left for Italy anyhow not knowing she wanted to recall what she could once see.

Thais did meet Gus because she got on the wrong train going to the city of L'Aquila. L'Aquila sits upon a hillside in the middle of a narrow valley surrounded by tall snow-capped mountains of the Gran Sasso.

At L'Aquila, while trying to arrange her way back to Rome, Thais had a short conversation with a blind woman who was on her way to the sheep herding village of Assergi. The blind woman was headed up to the mountains near Assergi to reach the spring of San Franco.

Thais didn't know about San Franco and she had never heard of the town of Assergi. Thais told the blind woman she must head back to Rome to ask about a man named Gus, and shared what little she knew about him. Thais could barely hide her surprise when the blind woman told her Gus was the man who gives directions to the spring and caves of San Franco, also more properly known as Saint Francisco Assergi.

It was a night filled with fog and few stars when Thais finally met Gus.

Perhaps it was her hair rolled under a men's motoring cap, instead of a scarf over her head, that led Gus to mistake Thais for a boy at first, despite her lissome figure.

"You are not here to find the path of Saint Francisco Assergi."

"No."

"You are not a boy. I was expecting to meet a boy."

"You were expecting me?"

"I was expecting to meet a boy."

"I get confused for a boy sometimes," Thais said, hopeful this information would alleviate the disappointment.

Gus wanted to say he knew but didn't care to speak unnecessarily.

Thais told her all that she had learned about the dark matter and Gus listened.

They sat quietly, not quite facing each other, breathing fog onto fog, for quite sometime.

"They still don't know what dark matter is," Thais said aloud, surprised at the sound of her own voice. She continued, "They may never find proof of it. But they know it exists. So they keep looking."

"Have you ever stood on a bridge and looked down?" Gus asked Thais instead.

"Yes."

"What do you see?"

"A reflection."

"Of?"

"The architecture, myself, everything. Depends how far away the bridge is from the body of water."

"The reflection is clear."

"No," replied Thais. Then she asked, unsure, "It is?"

Gus didn't answer.

"Depends on the water, I guess," said Thais.

"Depends what you are looking to see," replied Gus.

"You know what *that* is?" Thais jumped at the sudden movement by the old man as he reached his hand out and touched her stomach.

"My solar plexus," Thais said.

"*Here* there is a nerve plexus situated behind the stomach and in front of the aorta and the crura of the diaphragm, and it contains several ganglia distributing nerve fibers to the viscera," said Gus, pulling away his hand.

"The bridge between what you do and don't understand is the Soular Plexus of Spirit Nerves. That's the other dark matter."

Thais didn't sleep well that night and the following day, before leaving Assergi, she came to say goodbye to Gus.

"I suppose I go on looking for this bridge," Thais said, "not knowing if it even exists."

"Provando e riprovando," said the old man and then added, "you should know those aren't my words."

"Galileo said them, I know," Thais replied. She continued, "I also know it means 'experimenting and confirming.'"

"More accurately, 'trying and trying again'."

Thais began to understand the architecture of a search for something one may never find.

The search is the bridge, for dark matter within and without.

Jigar

The Persian and Urdu languages refer to the liver in figurative speech to indicate courage and strong feelings. The term *jan e jigar*, literally "the strength/life (power) of my liver," is a term of endearment in Urdu. In Persian slang jigar is used as an adjective for any object which is desirable, especially women. In the Zulu (South African) language, the word for liver (isibindi) is the same as the word for courage. The word liver originates from the Greek, Hepar.

> *The liver has always been an important symbol in occult physiology. As the largest organ, the one containing the most blood, it was regarded as the darkest, least penetrable part of man's innards. Thus it was considered to contain the secret of fate and was used for fortune-telling.*
> —James Hillman

A STORY HOLDS THAT A GIRL NAMED THAIS WAS BORN WITH A LIVER THE SIZE OF A CAMEL'S LIVER.

Those who know about Thais say she never loved anyone. There are others who say she loved everyone. Regardless of which story is told, all agree Thais loved with her liver, never her heart.

Everyone now knows, and even in the times of dirt roads foregone knew, the liver supports almost every organ in the body and is vital for survival. Because of its strategic location and multidimensional functions, the liver is also prone to many diseases. And because it is susceptible to much, the liver is the only internal human organ capable of natural regeneration of lost tissue: as little as twenty-five percent of a liver can regenerate into a whole liver.

Scientific and medical works about liver regeneration often refer to the Greek god Prometheus who was chained to a rock in the Caucasus where, each day, his liver was devoured by an eagle only to grow back each night. Some think the myth indicates that the ancient Greeks knew about the liver's remarkable capacity for self-repair, though this claim has been challenged.

The story of Thais, a young girl near Girga road in Egypt, is the primary reason for the aforementioned dispute. She lived among roads and caravan trails belonging to unknown communities in antiquity.

The Darb el-Arbain trade route, passing through Kharga in the south and Asyut in the north, was a long caravan route running north-south between Middle Egypt and the Sudan.

Thais was seventeen when she met a man and his camel on this road.

"Moira is my camel's name," the man told Thais.

He didn't say much else but told Thais she should meet him here at night if she wanted to know how to always protect her heart. Thais was alarmed and inquired why she should have to protect her heart.

"Because no one knows how to thermoregulate the temperature of love," he replied.

It would be many years later that Thais would learn that thermogenesis is the process of heat production in organisms.

"When you Love the heart produces immense heat to the object of affection—person or thing or place—which radiates through space and time. But just like Kleptothermy—"

"What is kleptothermy?" Thais asked.

"It is any form of thermoregulation,"

"What is thermoregulation?" Thais inquired.

"You know what it is. Regulation of body temperature."

Thais *did* know what that was. All of a sudden Thais felt the heavy burden of waves governed by the laws of memory move through her body.

"Anyway, kleptothermy is a way by which an animal shares in the metabolic thermogenesis of another animal. Heat borrowing."

Thais listened.

"Most heat-sharing is reciprocal," the man continued, "However, in at least one case this is not reciprocal, and might be accurately described as *heat-stealing*. Some male Canadian red-sided garter snakes engage in female mimicry by producing fake pheromones after emerging from hibernation. This causes rival males to cover them in a mistaken attempt to mate, and so transfer heat to them. This allows those males that mimic females to become more quickly revitalized after hibernation (which depends upon raising their body temperature), giving them an advantage in their own attempts to mate."

No one quite knows what happened that night, but Thais did meet the man and his camel. Some say she committed the sin of making love to a stranger who was neither her husband nor her lover. Some say the camel attacked her and she lost too much blood. Others claim the man assaulted her as would be expected.

Thais learned after that night that the most challenging temperature to regulate is that of love, for there exist those who steal the heat produced by love, the most important heat generated and sustained by the pendulum of reciprocity.

Her drawings that have been recovered show a different story but as with all lines drawn, the meaning is open to interpretation.

The stories born in the desert don't really belong to anyone. Her drawings are that of stars and camels.

When the pyramids were built, the star closest to the pole was Thuban, in Draco, the dragon. The stars close to the pole never set. The Egyptians described these stars as "imperishable" or "undying."

There are a number of myths behind the constellation Draco, due to its resemblance to a dragon, although alternative interpretations exist, such as the legend of the Mother Camels, the name given by ancient Arabic nomadic tribes to an asterism in the constellation of Draco. Instead of the head of a dragon, the asterism is interpreted as a ring of mother camels surrounding a baby camel (the faint star in the middle), with another mother camel running to join them. The camels were seen as protecting the baby from a line of charging hyenas.

Underneath these drawings is a caption that reads: "the heart is not capable of regenerating like the liver."

A Reflection from the Shore

OCEANS ARE NOT AS BLUE AS THEY APPEAR IN PIC-
TURES, Emilie Goldstein thought to herself, as she
looked at the loud waves reflecting the ashy, overcast
sky.

At the bony age of sixty-five Emilie Goldstein
considered herself, and made an effort to be perceived
as, an "attractive woman for her age." She justified her
demeanor, which barely bypassed the edge of narcis-
sism, due to all that she felt proud to have endured
physically and accomplished professionally. Wearing
Chanel's fire-engine-red lipstick shade, which appeared abnormally bright against her pale skin, matted
on her wrinkled mouth, made her feel put together
and powerful. She had read in a women's magazine
once that only the most confident of the professional
women wore red.

Emilie Goldstein was a breast-cancer survivor and
did not mind she had a severely hunched back; however, she was self-conscious about her staggered, slow
walk due to the needed hip replacement surgery and
arthritis in the lumbar joints. At her age, some would
say, including herself when she had herself convinced
without a doubt, she had it all: a life tenure court at-

torney position with the County Judge, a marriage of forty years, two sons in their late thirties who had yet to bear her grandchildren, company she considered friends with whom she had Wednesday manicures, Friday dinners every other week, Sunday brunches once a month, and opera and ballet once a year.

She sailed around the Long Island coast of North-Eastern Atlantic shore with her husband in the summers and enjoyed her inherited Miami apartment near South Beach every other Christmas.

Thursdays, during lunch, were reserved for herself to get her hair washed and set at a salon not far from the County Court.

Emilie Goldstein could never satisfy the longing to swim in the ocean for she never learned how to swim and she couldn't recall when she had decided it was too late to learn.

Prisoners of Life

I AM TWENTY-THREE YEARS OLD AND I AM IN PRISON. For life. Three strikes and you are out. Or should I say three strikes and you are "in"? I know, not funny. I like to crack jokes even when I know they are probably not funny. In my experience there is bound to be that one person that finds humor in something not funny. I like one-in-a-given-number statistics. Isn't that what life is? Chances. Choice is two letters away from Chance. Don't worry, I am not about to go all deep on you. I don't read that much in here like they always portray us doing.

I spend my time playing basketball and watching Court T.V. (didn't have cable growing up) and yes, sometimes I indulge in a little reading–mostly books on the law–it is some baffling shit. *Beyond a reasonable doubt* is subjective and you only tell yourself it is not, so you can go to sleep better at night.

I like playing a lot of basketball when the sun is out and we can step out in the court during yard time. Then I watch Court T.V. during dayroom time. Every 90 days I–we all–have to follow up with a psychiatrist and a psychologist, but I can request a follow up at any time. How much does your therapist cost? I am just playin' with you. Relax. I know I am afforded my many wonderful amenities here on your tax dollars. Wish my high school spent as much money on me as this prison does.

I don't play chess, but I like to watch others play when I am not playing basketball, even when the sun is out or there is nothing new on Court T.V.

My psychologist likes me because I told her this quote I had read: *"One cannot play chess if one becomes aware of the pieces as living souls and of the fact that the Whites and the Blacks have more in common with each other than with the players. Suddenly one loses all interest in who will be champion."* Anatol Rapoport said that. Among many other well-known books on fights, games, violence and peace, Rapoport analyzed contests in which there are more than two sets of conflicting interests, such as war, diplomacy, poker or bargaining.

My psychologist doesn't understand why I continued to make the choices I did which led me here–for good–for being a "fairly intelligent guy."

Do you understand why you are where you are?

I am twenty-three years old and I am in prison. You are not, right?

Attributions
and References

The following stories cite information from various Wikipedia articles.

"Love: Making Music"
"Kinein"
"Intuit"
"Memory of Silence"
"Inspiratus"
"Ferraris and Lamborghinis"
"Infinity's Muse"
"Reflection of Love"
"The Love of Your Life"
and the "Thais Stories"

The "Da Vinci Stories" were borne out of reading various NPR articles and Wikipedia definitions. Specifically, information about Capgras delusion in "Phantom Heart" was provided by "Seeing Imposters: When Loved Ones Suddenly Aren't" by Jad Abumrad and Robert Krulwich. (NPR. March, 30, 2010).

www.ingramcontent.com/pod-product-compliance
Lightning Source LLC
Chambersburg PA
CBHW050850180626
46814CB00007B/2708